What he saw defied all logic....

Andrew stared and wondered if he was hallucinating. Had he been underwater too long? Was he about to lose consciousness?

Because what he saw before him was a *mermaid*.... A mermaid with an enchanting oval face and long, floating golden hair. Through its shimmering, undulating strands he caught tantalizing glimpses of her voluptuous body, and his heart slammed against his ribs in disbelief.

She was only there for a few seconds. Then his light seemed to scare her off and she darted away from him.

Compelled by an urge beyond his control, he turned off the light and raced after the mermaid, frantic to catch up with her. Frantic to touch her, to find out if she could *possibly* be real.

He *had* to see her again!

Dear Reader,

The Mermaid Wife is the second book in my series about three wonderful Nevada heroes. The first was *The Rancher and the Redhead* (Harlequin Romance #3280, September 1993, and that month's Back to the Ranch title); the third will be *Bride of My Heart* (Harlequin Romance #3325), coming in August of this year.

This book's hero, Governor Andrew Cordell of Nevada, is pure fabrication and bears no resemblance to the present governor of that great state. However, I must extend my heartfelt thanks to the governor's staff; they patiently and graciously answered a multitude of questions, which has helped bring credence to my novel.

Another thank-you goes to Lucy Beth Rampton, wife of Utah's former governor, Calvin Rampton, for her insights about life as a first lady.

I would like to express my gratitude to Bruce, Linda, George and everyone else at Neptune Divers in Salt Lake for helping me with this book, for giving so generously of their time, expertise and facilities.

Also a huge thanks to Michael, Salt Lake's finest hairstylist, who loves to scuba dive and shared his information and experiences with me.

Finally, special thanks to Peter Krimley at the Bodega Marine Lab in California for telling me about sharks.

I hope you'll enjoy this romance between the governor and the mermaid. There's something about these fabled creatures of the deep that still fascinates us today. And while Lindsay isn't a *true* mermaid, she has a mermaid's knowledge of the ocean's secrets—and a mermaid's ability to enchant the hearts of men.

Sincerely,

Rebecca Winters

THE MERMAID WIFE

Rebecca Winters

Harlequin Books

TORONTO • NEW YORK • LONDON
AMSTERDAM • PARIS • SYDNEY • HAMBURG
STOCKHOLM • ATHENS • TOKYO • MILAN
MADRID • WARSAW • BUDAPEST • AUCKLAND

ISBN 0-373-03312-5

THE MERMAID WIFE

This edition published by arrangement with Harlequin Enterprises B. V.

Printed in U.S.A.

CHAPTER ONE

"GOOD JOB, you guys. Way to go! You keep this up and you'll beat the West Hollywood Club next Saturday hands down. Because *we've* got the best swimmers in the state of California."

Thirty-five boys and girls from ages six to seventeen cheered; thirty-five wet faces beamed up at Lindsay Marshall from the Olympic-size pool. She threw her long gold braid over her right shoulder and got down on one knee to talk to them.

"I'll be in the Bahamas for three weeks, but I should be back in time for the June twenty-seventh swim meet with Culver City. In the meantime, Bethany will be coaching you, so do everything she says. Any questions before the mothers' hour starts?"

"Yeah," a couple of the older teenage boys called out, "can we go with you?" Their question had the other children laughing uproariously.

Lindsay smiled into their bright eyes. "I wish I could take every one of you, but I'm afraid the people in charge of shooting the commercials would have something to say about that. I'm going there to work."

"Will it be dangerous?" little Cindy Lou asked. She was one of a dozen swimmers Lindsay coached on an individual basis, children who had special needs and required swim therapy. "I'd be afraid of sharks."

"You don't need to be because they don't bother people unless they're provoked. My biggest fear is that I might have to sneeze while I'm swimming around under twenty feet of water and my costume will burst at the seams."

"That wouldn't be bad at all," Kyle Roberts, the oldest swim-team member, commented while the rest of the kids laughed.

"Wise guy." Lindsay flashed him a grin and stood up. "Okay, everybody. Your lesson's over." She glanced at her watch, which read a little after five. "Oops. The mothers' hour started five minutes ago."

As everyone scrambled out of the pool, Lindsay stepped into her sandals, pulled on her T-shirt with the words Bel Air Club printed on the back and walked toward the office to put away her stopwatch and whistle.

"Hello, Nate," she said to the sun-bronzed lifeguard who'd covered for her in the office while she had given the swim team their lesson.

"Hello, yourself." His eyes swept over her long-legged curvaceous body in a way that made her skin crawl. Apparently a lot of women found nothing offensive in his behavior, though; they'd come out in droves since he'd been added to the staff in January. "You've had three phone calls, two of them from men. When are you going to break down and go out with *me?*"

Lindsay bit back the retort that formed on her lips. Being employed at this exclusive club, which catered to many of the Hollywood stars and their children, meant getting along with the other hired help—including has-been golf and tennis pros with their inflated sense of self-importance and Mr. Universe-type lifeguards whose biceps matched their bulging egos. "What are you, Nate—twenty-one, twenty-two?"

His smooth smile faded. "I'm twenty-four and you know it."

"Well, I'll be twenty-seven on my next birthday and I only date older men who aren't athletic. In other words, I don't go out with men who work here." It was actually the truth. The male specimens who worked at the club were so busy admiring themselves and hoping to be discovered by Hollywood talent scouts, no woman could possibly compete. "Thanks for asking, though, and thanks for taking my messages. See you at the end of the month."

Ignoring his sour look, she pulled the notes from the corkboard, reached for her purse and left the office. She waved to a couple of mothers she recognized as she went out to the parking lot. Her Jetta sat there—a bit forlornly, she thought—among the Ferraris, Mercedes, Jaguars and Porsches.

She glanced at the first message and saw Roger Bragg's name. He was the manager of the apartment complex next to hers, and she'd gone out on one date with him, which had been a big mistake. Before the evening was over, she'd discovered he was barely divorced and already talking to Lindsay about marrying her. Maybe while she was away he'd imagine himself in love with someone else.

The second message was from the travel agent who had arranged her flight and accommodations in Nassau. He'd called to say everything was confirmed and her ticket would be at the airline counter in the morning.

No doubt the third message was from her parents. Lindsay sighed, determined to avoid another argument about her taking a job they considered dangerous. The best course of action, she decided, would be to say goodbye to them from a pay phone at the L.A. airport before she boarded her flight.

Anxious to finish her packing and get away, Lindsay started the car and headed toward Santa Monica. The idea of swimming in the sunlit waters surrounding New Providence Island's famous marine park was a dream come true. Free diving in the clear azure waters of the Bahamas sounded like paradise after plunging into the cold seaweed-strewn ocean off the California coast.

Lindsay was immensely grateful to her best friend's mother for introducing her to the Hollywood agent who got her the starring role in the commercials for a new brand of cosmetics. She'd signed a ten-plus contract that would pay her agent's fee and give her $50,000. That money, combined with the small savings she'd accrued through her work at the club, would enable her to attend Scripp's Institute in San Diego as a full-time student in the fall. If she was frugal with her savings, she wouldn't have to worry about earning a living until she'd received her postgraduate degree.

The University of California at San Diego boasted one of the best oceanography schools in the world—Scripp's—and one day Lindsay intended to work on important environmental projects that would take her to various parts of the globe.

Since agreeing to do the commercials and signing the contract, she'd read everything she could find about swimming and diving in that part of the world; she'd also talked to countless scuba divers who had vacationed there. Everyone agreed those shallow waters, often referred to as the *baja mer,* were a sheer delight, and Lindsay could hardly wait to explore the dive sites in what was regarded as one of the world's greatest maritime highways.

Descriptions of the Spanish galleons and pirate ships that had sailed those waters, and the reefs, corals and tropical fish that existed there had ignited her already lively imagination. She had one week before the actual filming began to swim in the area designated for the commercial and to practice the underwater routines. She'd already walked through them on stage with the director and choreographer at the studio.

When she wasn't rehearsing, she planned to make use of every second of her free time. She particularly wanted to dive what was called The Buoy, a two-mile vertical expanse of clear blue where the dive master baits the water to bring in sharks. Lindsay could get as close as she wanted to those fascinating creatures. She knew it would be difficult to come back to California after such an experience.

Only the promise of her future career, which would give her the independence she craved, made thoughts of her return to Santa Monica bearable.

ANDREW CORDELL walked into Randy's bedroom and gave a wolf whistle when he saw his eighteen-year-old son parading around in a new black-and-pink wet suit complete with mask, boots and flippers. Randy had purchased it for their upcoming vacation in the Bahamas.

"Cut that out, Dad." Randy grinned and tossed a sack at his unsuspecting father, who caught it in one deft movement. "You told me to go ahead and buy the gear we'd need, so I picked us out identical outfits. They're perfect for the temperature of the water down there. Put yours on and let's see how it fits."

Andrew's mouth quirked. "Since I trust your judgment, I think I'll pass until we arrive in Nassau tomorrow."

"Hey, Dad, you don't need to be embarrassed. For a thirty-seven-year-old guy who's over the hill, you still look pretty rad."

Andrew's dark blond eyebrows lifted in mock surprise. "Did I hear you correctly? Did my one and only offspring deign to praise me for something?"

"Yeah. In fact Linda, the other diving instructor, has the hots for you."

"Linda? I don't recall her."

"It's a good thing she didn't hear you say that. She's constantly badgering me for information about my famous father every time she comes in to give a lesson. She says you remind her of a younger Robert Redford, but you're better-looking. Those are her exact words. I swear." He gestured with his hands. "Aunt Alex said almost exactly the same thing in front of Uncle Zack when we drove up to Hidden Lake last year, and he almost went off the road."

"Is that so?" Andrew chuckled, still bemused by the fact that his brother-in-law, Zackery Quinn, Nevada's most confirmed bachelor until Alexandria Duncan had come along, was now ecstatically married. Zack was so much in love he could hardly bear to let his beautiful, pregnant, redheaded wife out of his sight.

"Yeah." Randy flashed him another quick smile reminiscent of Wendie's. Andrew felt the familiar pang of loss that still came to him at odd moments, even though his wife had been dead three years. "How about your packing? Have you even started?"

Andrew darted his son a sheepish glance. "I thought you might like to come to my room and help me. I'm afraid that—"

"You're afraid that the meeting with your department heads went longer than you expected. You had a lot of business to clear up because we'll be gone for two weeks." Randy took the words out of his father's mouth, but he spoke with teasing warmth.

Andrew smiled at his dark-haired son, who stood only an inch shorter than Andrew's six foot three, realizing as never before how much he loved him. He was proud of Randy, too, for taking an after-school job at the scuba shop and going to diving classes in the evenings, classes he paid for with his own earnings. Randy had managed to certify for open-water diving; in fact, he liked it so much, he'd talked Andrew into certifying, too.

Grasping any opportunity to spend time with his son, Andrew had taken the six-week course in the spring, never dreaming he'd become addicted to the sport. It was the incredible feeling of weightlessness he loved. But even more important, diving relied heavily on the buddy system, which helped bring the two of them even closer together.

Now that it was June, and Randy had graduated from high school, Andrew was as excited as his son to be going off on their first real underwater adventure—Andrew's graduation present to Randy—and leaving the burdens of his political office behind. "I can hardly wait." And he meant it.

"Yeah. Me, too," Randy replied with a catch in his throat. He peeled off his wet suit and placed it in the gear bag on his bed. "It's a good thing we're heading out of the country, otherwise your work would get in the way no matter how hard you tried to ignore it." He pulled on a T-shirt and shorts. "It's true what everyone says about you, you know."

He followed his father out the door and down the hall to the master bedroom on the top floor of the governor's mansion in Carson City. "You do work too hard. It's about time you had a real vacation that doesn't have to be combined with business."

"I couldn't agree with you more," Andrew murmured. He knew Randy's comment was well-meaning, but the truth hurt. It reminded Andrew how little time he'd had for his son since becoming governor of the state of Nevada. And Wendie's death halfway through his first term of office had only made things worse. His own grief had been too deep to help Randy deal with the loss of his mother, let alone the other adjustments faced by an adolescent suddenly living in the public eye.

As a result, Randy had gotten into serious trouble, something the media had pounced on and exploited with relish. But it took Randy's escapade with Troy Duncan, Alex's now eighteen-year-old brother, to jolt Andrew to an awareness of his failure as a father.

Randy had met Troy over ham radio the summer before, and they'd quickly become involved in an illegal mail-order business—selling pictures of Troy's sister, Alex. Pictures she didn't even know about....

An ever-loyal Zack had uncovered the boys' guilty secret and prevented it from reaching the headlines while Andrew was out of the country on a State Department tour. Andrew had finally been forced to deal with the painful truth.

Unintentionally, he'd been partially responsible for his son's unhappiness since Wendie's death. His late father-in-law's favorite adage "No success compensates for failure in the home" resounded loudly in his ears. Naturally he'd wanted to be successful, but more than that, it was his desire to honor his campaign promises, to be the man who got the job done, that drove him so relentlessly. And he'd been able to submerge his grief in the long hours and hard work.

He had become estranged from his son, had forgotten to honor his own fatherhood, the most important commitment of all. But since that revealing night eleven months ago—when a repentant Randy had come to him without any prompting from Zack, telling him about his ill-advised mail-order business and begging his father's forgiveness—Andrew had become a changed man.

He'd begged Randy to forgive *him* for the waste of precious time. Because of his own demanding agenda, he had unwittingly excluded his son. They'd wept together, and from that moment on a healing had taken place. They'd vowed to put their relationship above all else. And from that day, neither of them had ever let anything come between them.

"Son? Did I tell you what Jim has arranged for us?" he asked, choosing one of his lightweight suits in a pale gray to pack for the trip.

"You mean besides letting us use his house?"

"He called me from his office in Sacramento a couple of days ago and told me a seaplane would be waiting to fly us from Miami to Nassau Harbor. Sounds like fun, doesn't it? Making a landing on the water?"

"It sounds awesome! You and Governor Stevens must be good friends."

"We hit it off when we went on that tour last summer. He and Mary have two daughters, seventeen and nineteen, and I've invited the family to stay here with us for a few weeks in July."

Randy eyed his father with growing interest. "Have you met his daughters?"

"No." Andrew grinned. "But I've seen pictures and they're both very attractive. I'm counting on you and Troy to show them around here and Virginia City, introduce them to your friends, take them riding on the Circle Q. Think you might be able to handle that?" He tried to keep a poker face while he picked out a few ties.

"Yeah." Randy laughed. "Dad, if you don't need me anymore, I've got something important to do."

"It's a good thing you and Troy have ham sets," Andrew called over his shoulder. "Otherwise you'd have to work weekends and overtime to afford the phone bills between here and the Circle Q. Good night, Randy. Don't forget to set your alarm."

"Who needs an alarm? I'm so excited about this trip I won't be able to get to sleep. Oh, by the way,

Uncle Zack called and said he and the family will be by at six-thirty in the morning to drive to the airport with us."

"Great. Now go get some rest."

"I'll try, but I won't promise anything. Good night, Dad."

Still smiling, Andrew made a couple of last-minute phone calls to clear up some loose ends, then finished his packing. When he finally got into bed and reached over to turn off the light, he came face-to-face with Wendie's picture propped on the bedside table and stared at it in surprise.

For the first time since her death, he'd forgotten to pack it with his things. A part of him felt a twinge of guilt for that small betrayal. But another part realized that somewhere along the way, he'd stopped mourning her. He wondered when it had happened, when he'd finally let her go....

"BETH, I SHOULDN'T HAVE let you drive me to the airport—I know how much you love to sleep in. But I'm thankful you did. It's been good to talk. Mom and Dad have been impossible about this trip."

Her best friend pulled the car to a stop in front of the terminal and turned to her. "They'll always be impossible until they get counseling. But until that day comes, my advice is to fly to Nassau and enjoy yourself. Think of all those fabulous balmy nights and moonlit beaches with gorgeous bronzed hunks walking along the surf hoping to meet someone like you."

Lindsay's brows arched. "I see enough of those at the club. I'm going there to work, remember?" She got out of Bethany's convertible and pulled her suitcase from the back seat, then walked around to the driver's side and gave her friend a hug. "Thanks for everything. I don't know how I would have made it through life this far without you."

"That's what I'm always saying to you," Beth murmured. "Three weeks is a long time. Phone me, or I'll go crazy wondering how you are."

"I'll call, but you'll probably be out with Doug. Maybe you should phone me because I'll be in my room every night after work, exhausted."

"Want to bet? Listen to me, Lindsay Marshall. You're like a light shining on a hill. You draw men whether you mean to or not. And once the commercials hit television, you'll be touted as the Esther Williams of the nineties, and the contracts will come pouring in. Men will swoon at your feet and I'll *never* see you again."

Lindsay chuckled." You of all people know the life of a movie star holds absolutely no allure for me. I'm doing this *one*-time job for the money. It's so I can go to graduate school, nothing else. I don't have time for men right now."

"Famous last words," Beth called over her shoulder as she drove away from the terminal curb with a speed only L.A. drivers could manage without an accident. Lindsay waved until her friend's car was out of sight, then walked through the terminal doors to check in and board her flight.

Once the jet was airborne, she pulled out a new mystery novel and settled back to enjoy it. But the unresolved problem with her parents prevented her from concentrating and she put the book down to stare out the window.

Her parents had been calling her apartment every day for the past week, begging her not to take this job. Only yesterday evening, her father had phoned to say that her mother was in bed with a severe migraine—which was his way of bringing pressure to bear.

But none of their ploys to prevent her from moving out of their house two years ago had done any good, and she refused to be manipulated now. Much as she loved them and knew they loved her, she felt smothered by their affection and concern. For the hundredth time she found herself wishing they'd had more children on whom to lavish their attention.

The fact that she was an only child made them more protective than most parents. But Lindsay knew that a very understandable fear for her safety lay at the root of their problem. Once, several months ago, she'd suggested they talk to a professional about their concerns, but this had only created more alienation and hurt feelings, so Lindsay had never mentioned it again.

Until she was eleven, life had been fairly normal at the Marshall home. Then Lindsay had gone on her first outing with a group of girls. Their bus and a semitrailer had collided in the mountains, sending several children to the hospital.

Lindsay's lower spine had been injured, and it had taken several operations and years of therapy before she could walk again. For a long time she'd had to be tutored at home. If it hadn't been for the companionship of Beth, and Beth's mother, Lindsay would have suffered from boredom and loneliness.

Her father and mother, a successful screenwriting duo, worked at home, where they were constantly on hand to provide encouragement—which all too often took the form of hovering.

When the doctor recommended swimming as an excellent form of therapy, her parents had a pool built and hired a swimming coach and a physical therapist to aid their daughter's recovery. Their good intentions and their love couldn't be questioned. But their overprotectiveness had its origins in that accident.

By the time she was ready for college, she could walk normally again, with only some scars on her back to remind her of her horrible ordeal. Lindsay would have been ecstatic over her recovery, except that her parents still continued to treat her as if she were an eleven-year-old invalid. They didn't want her out of their sight and insisted she attend college close to home.

Because she was so grateful for their concern, so aware that they'd given years of their lives to see that she regained the use of her limbs, Lindsay complied with their wishes. Knowing how much they worried when she went off with other students, Lindsay more often than not entertained her friends at home to keep her parents happy.

It wasn't until Greg Porter came on the scene during her junior year in college that she saw the situation for what it was. He'd invited her to vacation with him and his family at their beach house in La Jolla. Her parents were adamant in their refusal to let her go, saying that unless she and Greg were engaged, it was out of the question. Not even Greg's parents could persuade them to relent.

Short of defying her mother and father, something she'd never done, Lindsay had to refuse Greg's invitation. Eventually he found someone else, and this started a pattern that continued until she graduated from college with a degree in biology—and a series of aborted romantic relationships. In retrospect, she could see they'd been sabotaged by her parents, though Helen and Ned Marshall had never seen it that way.

When they categorically refused to hear of her going away to graduate school to study marine biology, Lindsay confided in her best friend. Beth was in therapy to help her cope with the fourth marriage of her famous actress mother, an insecure woman Lindsay loved very much. Beth's response was to tell Lindsay that the Marshall family was "dysfunctional," and they all needed psychiatric help.

At first, Lindsay didn't want to hear it and resented Beth's remarks. But in time she realized her friend was right. That was when Lindsay applied for a part-time job as a children's swimming instructor at the local club to pay for visits to a good psychiatrist.

Four months of therapy turned Lindsay's world around, and though she couldn't do anything about her parents' fears, she could help herself. Using the strategy outlined by her psychiatrist, Lindsay was finally able to make the break. She found herself an apartment in Santa Monica close to the beach, where she could swim daily in the surf and take scuba lessons for open-water certification.

Living in Santa Monica gave Lindsay breathing room, yet she was close enough to Bel Air to assure her parents she hadn't abandoned them.

They immediately cut off all money, hoping that when she ran out, she'd come back home. But being on her own was a liberating experience for Lindsay. She put her plans for graduate school on temporary hold and went to work full time at the club as a swimming instructor and lifeguard to support herself. As her reputation for coaching children with deformities, cerebral palsy and spinal injuries grew, she was asked to take on additional classes, which allowed her to augment her income. She made an adequate living and managed to save a little money each month.

Best of all, she was free to make her own mistakes and decisions. When her parents realized their tactics weren't working they became even more manipulative, playing on her feelings of guilt. Her father's call the night before was typical. But Lindsay had been on her own too long and was too excited by the prospect of traveling to the Caribbean to be swayed by their arguments.

All she could do was continue to love them and stay in touch as much as possible. Maybe in time they'd get over the worst of their obsessive fears.

Except for her parents, everyone Lindsay knew, particularly Beth, thought a career in marine biology sounded like a great idea. Beth predicted she'd end up marrying a marine biologist like herself and living a life of semiseclusion in some remote area of the world.

But a husband was the last thing on Lindsay's mind. She had no intention of placing herself in a position where she could be controlled or manipulated—especially when she was still battling the problem with her parents. Her freedom meant everything.

CHAPTER TWO

"HEY, DAD! How about doing one more short dive at 20,000 Leagues before we go back to the house for dinner? I want to see if I can get pictures of that queen angelfish we saw a couple of days ago."

This would be their third dive of the day. They'd already visited the Cessna Wreck and the so-called Bond Wrecks, where several James Bond movies had been filmed. Yet Randy could never get enough, and if the truth be known, neither could Andrew.

They'd explored 20,000 Leagues on their first day in the Bahamas, during an inshore twenty-five-foot-dive off the Clifton Wall. It boasted a coral garden with twisting channels that afforded spectacular views of tropical fish and the larger Nassau groupers, and they both wanted to see it again.

Andrew turned in the seat of the flattop boat and nodded to the robust dive master, Pokey Albright, and his crew. Natives of New Providence, they'd all been checked out long before Andrew's arrival in Nassau and had acted as their guides, accompanying them on every dive. "Let's do it, Pokey." At Andrew's words, the jovial, red-bearded man gave instructions to the driver, and they headed toward their destination at full speed.

As they skimmed across the sparkling waters, Andrew saw Skip and Larry, his two security men, grimace. They'd been out twice that day already and were probably bored to distraction. He wished that being governor didn't mean acquiring bodyguards who went everywhere he did, whether he was working or vacationing. They even kept an all-night vigil outside his bedroom door. But the escalation of violent crime in the past decade had made it imperative that he be protected.

After five years, Andrew was used to his shadows and had learned to live with them. So had Randy. But Andrew knew that for Skip and Larry, this was security work at its worst. While the Cordells were having the time of their lives, the other two men had to remain in the hot boat for hours on end, guarding against any unforeseen circumstances.

For this vacation Andrew had brought along six security men. One of them remained at the dock while the other three were stationed at the vacation retreat located in the exclusive Lyford Cay development on the south side of the island—which had its own set of tough-looking security guards.

Even surrounded by security, Andrew had already experienced trouble with the press. One photographer had gotten close enough to take a picture as he and Randy alighted from the limo after they'd reached the airport in Reno. And despite heavy security after their seaplane had landed in Nassau Harbor, someone from the tabloids—dressed like an airline official—had suddenly produced a camera.

Both pictures had appeared in American newspapers the next day, informing the world that the governor of Nevada and his son were on vacation in the Caribbean. Since it was impossible to know what some "crazy" might do with that information, Andrew was forced to take every precaution. But at least while they were diving, Andrew and Randy could leave all those cares behind and enter an underwater world of incredible beauty. Below the surface they were totally anonymous and free to swim among the fish in delightful eighty-degree waters.

When the boat finally came to a stop, Andrew could see only one other dive boat far off in the distance. At five in the afternoon, it seemed most people had finished diving for the day. They had the place virtually to themselves—which would give Skip and Larry a break.

At this point Andrew and Randy knew the routine by heart. They checked their gauges while Pokey helped them figure out their diving tables, deciding they could stay down for twenty-five minutes.

Andrew caught the flash of challenge in Randy's eyes as they started to dress. It was a game between them to see who could hit the water first. Determined to win at least once to prove he wasn't *that* far over the hill, Andrew pulled on his wet suit with lightning speed. Then he put on boots and fins and fastened the weight belt around his waist. Next he checked the air pressure to make sure he had a full tank before donning his buoyancy control device, or BCD. After that came the regulator and mask, and he was ready with video camera in hand.

To his delight Randy was still struggling to make the skirt of his mask fit properly, which gave Andrew the lead. Signaling to Pokey, he made his way to the edge of the boat and jumped overboard, well away from the mooring pennant.

Every time Andrew entered the water, he experienced a thrill of excitement. It sent a rush of adrenaline through his body, and he had to remember to stay calm and breathe normally as he began his descent. In one of his early diving lessons, he'd forgotten the rule about not holding his breath—a mistake that ultimately results in death. Fortunately he'd never done that again.

When he reached the twenty-foot level, he achieved neutral buoyancy by controlling his breathing, then turned to capture Randy's and Pokey's descent on videotape. They drifted slowly down, past walls of spurs rising ten feet from serpentine sand channels.

Andrew had read that diving the 20,000 Leagues was like surveying the Grand Canyon by helicopter. Since he'd done that very thing with Governor Knox of Arizona a couple of years back, he could definitely concur with the author's description. Every twist and turn of the narrow gullies provided a new vista of spurs or a spectacular new view of tropical fish resting and feeding in the crevices and undercuts of the reef.

Pokey made a hand signal, and for the next ten minutes they followed him through the chutes, some so tight they had to be careful their fins didn't touch the fragile coral. When they reached the edge of the wall, a large leopard ray moved unexpectedly into view.

Andrew used up most of the videotape on Randy and Pokey as they swam within touching distance of the ray. It hovered over the sandy bottom, then quickly propelled itself off again. Pokey made the sign for them to follow him once more.

With Andrew bringing up the rear, they moved single file through more curving channels, keeping no farther than twenty feet apart for safety's sake. But suddenly Andrew saw something large coming at him through a gully on his left. He slowed to a stop, thinking it must be a jumbo grouper. The reef was famous for them, and he'd caught the glint of a distinctive fin.

His pulse pounded with excitement as he lifted the camera into position and turned on the light. But what he saw through the lens defied all logic and made him think he was hallucinating.

A mermaid. A breathtaking mermaid with an enchanting oval face and long golden hair floating around her graceful arms and shoulders. Through the shimmering, undulating strands he caught tantalizing glimpses of her voluptuous body, and his heart slammed against his ribs in stunned disbelief.

She was only there for brief seconds. Then the light seemed to scare her off, and she darted away from him with incredible speed.

Compelled by an urge beyond his control, he turned off the light and raced after her, frantic to catch up with her. Frantic to touch her, to find out if anything that hauntingly beautiful could be real.

He hadn't gone thirty feet before he heard the sound of someone tapping on his tank. Disoriented, he looked around and saw Pokey pointing at his watch, then lifting his thumbs to indicate it was time to go up.

Dear Lord. For a few seconds he'd actually forgotten Pokey and Randy. For that matter, he'd forgotten where he was or what he was doing. The sight of the mermaid had driven every other thought from his head. Maybe he'd done too much diving in one day and was in the last stages of consciousness before blacking out.

When they reached the fifteen-foot level, Pokey extended his palm, which meant stop. He wrote on a slate hanging from a lanyard attached to his front clip, "Already gone up with Randy. You went over your bottom time. We'll have to wait here 3 minutes. Make the OK sign if you understand me."

Andrew had felt like a fool many times in his life, but this experience had to be one of the worst. Red-faced with embarrassment, he made the correct signal with his right hand, all the while imagining Pokey's disgust. After this experience, he wouldn't be surprised if the dive master refused to take him on any more dives. And he knew that Randy would be sitting up in that boat wondering why his dad hadn't surfaced with Pokey and him and feeling more anxious by the second.

Pokey wrote another message, "Are you OK?"

Andrew reached for the slate and wrote, "Yes." If he tried to explain that he'd seen a mermaid, Pokey would think he'd lost his mind. And maybe he had....

What was wrong with him? He'd never acted so foolishly in his life! Until he could get back to the house and watch the video to see if his mermaid was fact or fiction, he'd say nothing about the incident.

Deciding he'd better make some explanation he wrote, "I was taping and forgot the time. Sorry! Thanks for helping me."

After reading the slate Pokey wrote, "Same thing happened to me when I first started to dive. Forget it."

That'll be impossible, Andrew mused, still dazed and shaken by what he thought he'd seen. He was growing more and more impatient to view the video. If nothing showed up except tropical fish and coral, he would consult an expert in diving medicine to find out what had caused his hallucination. He couldn't recall his instructor mentioning this kind of symptom when a diver got into trouble.

When the three minutes had passed, they rose to the surface and Andrew saw the look of relief that crossed Randy's face as he took the camera from him and helped him into the boat. Skip and Larry appeared equally upset.

"Jeez Dad, what happened? Are you all right?"

Andrew took off his mask and undid his BCD, setting it on the floor of the boat. "I'm fine, Randy." He flung an arm around his son's shoulders to give him a reassuring hug.

Pokey grinned at them. "Your dad just got a little too excited over the view down there and forgot to stop taping."

Excited wasn't the word. Something had happened to him while he was down there, something that had never happened to him before.

Andrew could tell his son was still apprehensive. "I was afraid maybe you'd had a heart attack or something," Randy admitted in a surprisingly unsteady voice. It made Andrew feel like hell. He *could* have died—and it would have been due to his own carelessness. After losing his mother, Randy didn't need another tragedy in his young life.

"I know thirty-seven sounds ancient to you, but before we left home I had a complete physical, and the doctor told me I was in A1 shape." He peeled off his wet suit. "Forgive me for scaring you, Randy. I'll never be that stupid again."

"Promise?" He sounded as if he'd recovered, but his eyes still looked haunted and his face had paled.

He squeezed Randy's shoulders. "I swear it."

"Okay then." The ghost of a smile broke the corner of Randy's mouth.

Andrew heaved a sigh and nodded to Pokey. "Let's go home. I'm starving. What's the best restaurant in Nassau? I think Randy and I are in the mood to be extravagant."

"That'll be the Graycliff on West Hill Street, especially if you like seafood." This came from the boat driver.

"How about it, Randy?"

"Sounds good to me," he replied, but without his usual enthusiasm.

More than anything, Andrew wanted to reassure his son, but he needed total privacy when he talked to him. And until he had a rational explanation for what he'd seen, it might be better to say nothing.

"Did you find your queen angel?" the driver asked Randy as he started the boat and headed for port. Even he could tell that Randy wasn't himself, and Andrew felt grateful to the man for trying to lighten the mood.

"No," Pokey answered for him, "we saw something better, didn't we?" He tousled Randy's hair and proceeded to describe the leopard ray.

When they reached shore, the security man Andrew had left at the dock was standing by with the bullet-proof limousine. Andrew turned to thank Pokey and the driver for the great diving day, adding that he'd call them in the morning when he and Randy knew their plans.

Right now he couldn't think about anything beyond watching that video!

Leaving all their diving gear in the boat, Andrew followed Randy into the limousine, clutching the camera in his hand. They drove quickly back to Lyford Cay, where his other security men greeted them.

The minute they entered the Grecian-styled villa with its cool white walls and flowering plants, a taciturn Randy disappeared, telling his father he was going to take a shower.

Relieved to be alone, Andrew strode directly to the master bedroom, which had a TV and VCR. Still dressed in his swim trunks and thongs, he removed the tape from the camera and put it in the machine, rewinding it partway. Then he pulled a chair close to the TV and sat down to watch.

The shots of the airplane wreck looked sensational, but Andrew would study those later; he pressed fast forward. When he released it, he saw Randy floating above the ray, getting as close as he dared without touching it.

As Andrew watched and waited, beads of perspiration broke out on his forehead and upper lip. His heartbeat accelerated with excitement and anxiety. Suddenly, there she was! He leapt to his feet.

"Yes!" he cried with such force two security men flung open the bedroom door as if expecting trouble.

"I'm just enjoying the video of today's dives." He laughed so joyously they looked perplexed and apologized for disturbing him. As soon as they closed the door, Andrew got down on his knees in front of the screen, then rewound the film, stopping when he got to a close-up. He pressed the pause button and took a long hard look.

She was exquisite, an enchanting sea goddess whose golden hair floated about her like a cloud. His presence had obviously startled her. Her dark-fringed eyes beneath delicately arched brows were wide open, their amethyst color as exotic as the schools of fluorescent fish. Her heart-shaped mouth formed a small O, causing an air bubble to escape.

His gaze moved lower to the swell of her full rounded curves partially confined by a pale pink bikini top. Then his eyes fell to her slender waist and the barely visible flare of her hips. If he'd caught up with her, he would have touched warm firm flesh....

Andrew's pulses were in chaos. Was he losing his mind? He'd never responded to a woman like this before in his life. Not even meeting Wendie had produced the rush of exhilaration he was experiencing now. What was the matter with him?

After taking several deep steadying breaths, he released the pause button. Immediately she darted away. He gazed at the long curving lines of her hips and legs, encased in a mermaid tail that fastened around her waist. He wanted to reach right through the screen and close his hands around those enticing hips before she disappeared into the blue. And then he wanted to—

"Dad? You haven't even showered yet!"

Randy's voice jerked Andrew back to reality. Hot-faced, he got to his feet and tried to slow the frantic beating of his heart. He rewound the tape to give himself time to recover. "I couldn't wait to see the video I shot of you today."

Randy moved closer. "Is it any good?" he asked, sounding more like the Randy who'd been so excited about this trip.

"Better than good," Andrew murmured, then turned to face his son.

Randy stared at his father. "Dad? Are you all right?"

"Of course. Why wouldn't I be?"

"I don't know. Ever since you surfaced, you just seem . . . different."

A slow smile lit Andrew's face. "Son, do you believe in mermaids?"

Randy's head jerked back and he laughed. *"Mermaids?"*

"You know what I mean. Those fantastic half woman half fish creatures who lure sailors to their doom."

"Yeah." Randy grinned back. "They're too gorgeous to be real."

Andrew folded his arms across his broad chest. "Do you want to make a bet?"

Randy's brows furrowed in puzzlement. "Dad, you're not making sense."

"Then maybe this will clarify things for you. Stay right where you are." Andrew rewound the tape a little, then let it play. Randy made sounds of excitement as he watched himself and Pokey swimming above the ray. But the moment the mermaid flashed onto the screen, the room fell silent and Randy watched as if hypnotized.

"Jeez..." When she'd disappeared, Andrew pressed the stop button, then lifted his head. His eyes met his son's in silent communication.

"I don't believe what I just saw," Randy whispered. "Dad, she's *more* than gorgeous, she's..." He seemed to be searching for the right word, gesturing with his hands.

Andrew gave his son a wry smile and nodded. "I know. Now maybe you'll understand what prevented me from following you to the surface. I thought I was hallucinating."

"Let me see that again!" Randy reached in front of his father to rewind the tape. Like Andrew, he pressed the pause button when her face appeared directly in front of the camera, then he let out a low whistle. "No wonder you took so long. If I'd been you, I'd have probably stopped breathing and be dead by now."

Andrew stood behind Randy to watch. "I hesitated telling you and Pokey the truth until I could see the tape, because I was afraid you wouldn't believe me. And to be honest, I worried that maybe there was something wrong with me."

"What I'd give to still be in the mail-order business. With a poster of her, Troy and I could be millionaires. Wait'll he gets a load of this!"

Andrew chuckled. Trust Randy to bring that up now.

"Dad, who do you think she is? And what do you suppose she was doing down there dressed in that costume without scuba gear?"

"I don't know," Andrew murmured, deep in thought. "But I'm going to find out."

Randy wheeled around and eyed his father speculatively. "Yeah?"

"Yeah," Andrew mimicked his son. "Can you blame me?"

"Heck no. I only wish I'd seen her first!"

"Well, you didn't, so hands off," came the gruff warning.

"That's an interesting choice of words, Dad," Randy said with uncanny perception. "My gosh, there's life in the old man yet."

Andrew chuckled again. "Remember what Bruce told us about salvage?"

Randy nodded. "Sure I do. What we find, we keep. But I wouldn't exactly describe her as salvage, Dad."

"Oh, I don't know." He rewound the tape and turned off the machine. "I found her under the water, free and unencumbered. Taking her away doesn't constitute any danger to the environment. And she could be worth a fortune. Who knows until I've examined her?"

"Dad..." Randy stared at his father through new eyes. "You've got the hots for her! I don't believe it. My own father!"

Andrew planted his hands on his hips. "How do you suppose you were conceived?"

"If this is your way of giving me a refresher course in sex education, you're at least five years too late. So how are you going to go about finding her?"

"Pokey knows everything that's happening in these waters. I'll phone him after we get back from dinner.

I just hope he's in, or I'll have to wait until morning."

"That means you'll lie awake all night going nuts, and you won't be any good for diving tomorrow. Why don't we stay in tonight so you can talk to him? I'll order pizza and pick up a video. I'm actually pretty tired—I'd just as soon relax around here."

"I know you're lying through your teeth to appease your old man. But under the circumstances, I'll take you up on your offer."

Randy laughed and shook his head. "Now I know why I went crazy over Aunt Alex's picture the first time I saw it. You know what they say. Like father, like son."

"It seems to run in the family, all right."

"Yeah, and Uncle Zack is the worst. Did you know he kept all those posters of Aunt Alex in his room after he took them away from me? He didn't destroy them like we thought."

"You're kidding." Andrew grinned. "Do you know that for sure?"

"His housekeeper told me. Yolanda saw them while she was cleaning his room. That's when she figured he'd be getting married soon. Wouldn't that be something if *you* ended up marrying your mystery woman? I can see the headlines now: Governor Takes Mermaid for First Lady."

"Get out of here, Randy, and don't come back without a large pizza for me. Everything on it except anchovies."

Whistling tunelessly, Andrew searched for Pokey's number among the pile of brochures and papers on the bedside table. He managed to reach one of the people in the dive shop, who told him Pokey was still out in the boat but was expected back shortly. Andrew left a message for Pokey to return his call as soon as he could.

Andrew had no idea how long he'd have to wait, so he left the bathroom door open and took a quick shower. Just as he stepped out, still wet, the phone rang. He hitched a towel around his hips and dashed into the other room to answer it. Pokey's voice came over the line.

"Bryan told me to call you, Governor. Do you have a question about tomorrow's dive?"

"No. There's something else on my mind, and I need your help." Without wasting words, he explained about the mermaid and asked Pokey what, if anything, he knew.

"A lot of film crews come down here to make movies and commercials. I know that 20,000 Leagues is going to be the location for a crew arriving on Monday. They'll be shooting underwater scenes there for a week—some kind of TV commercial—then they're going to spend another week at Thunderball Reef.

"They give the dive shops advance notice so we can keep divers away from the sites as much as possible. Maybe the woman you saw was rehearsing her part. That late in the day, she probably figured she'd have the place to herself. Come to think of it, there was another dive boat speeding away from our general area when I surfaced with Randy."

"Could it have been one of yours?"

"No, but I can call around and give you the info you want within an hour or two."

"If you can get me the name and address of that woman, you'll receive a bonus on top of your fee."

"I'll do my best. Are you going to be home or out for the next while?"

"We're not going to dinner, after all. Call anytime. And Pokey...remember, this is strictly confidential."

"I hear you. Don't worry. In this business you learn to keep a secret."

"Thanks," Andrew said.

When he'd hung up, he went back to the bathroom to finish toweling himself off and put on his robe. After that, he sat in front of the TV and watched the video from start to finish, thrilled with what he'd captured and more enamored of the mermaid than ever. He rewound the film, watching her again, still trying to figure out *why* he felt so...so compulsively drawn to this woman. It was a feeling that went far beyond mere attraction.

"Aha! Caught you in the act! Good grief, Dad, have you ever got it bad," Randy observed from the doorway. "In case you're interested, I'm back with the food." Randy crossed to his father and put the pizzas and drinks on the credenza next to the TV. "The video selections were lousy, but I got one I know you'll like."

"If it's *The Deep* again, I'll pass."

"You're getting warm."

"Same thing goes for *Jaws* one through a hundred."

"Warmer still."

"*20,000 Leagues Under the Sea?* We saw that before we left for Nassau."

"Nope. This is one I guarantee you've never seen before. Sit back and enjoy." Randy ejected the other tape and put in the movie he'd rented. Then he pulled up a chair next to Andrew and they both started eating.

The second Andrew saw the title appear on the screen his chuckle grew into genuine laughter. Randy gave him a sheepish grin. "If you promise not to tell anyone, I watched *The Little Mermaid* with Steve while he was baby-sitting his little sister. For a cartoon, it's really good."

For the next hour Andrew sat there, not having the least difficulty understanding the prince's desire to find the lovely mermaid who had enchanted him. In fact it was embarrassing to realize how similar his reaction to the sight of the mermaid had been to the prince's.

The phone rang while the prince was being urged to "Kiss the Girl." It was Pokey. "You're in luck, Governor. Don, one of the dive masters over on the west end of the island, has spent most of this week with your mermaid. Her name is Lindsay Marshall. She's twenty-six, single, and she's from Santa Monica, California. She's going to be the star in the commercial I was telling you about, the one they're shooting next week. It's for a new line of beauty products made from ocean materials like seaweed. 'Beauty from the Sea,' they're calling it."

"Where's she staying?" Andrew asked, trying to keep the excitement out of his voice.

"Everyone connected with the commercial is putting up at the Black Coral Marina Hotel on the west end. Apparently she practices free diving at Thunderball Reef as early as six-thirty in the morning and then again at five in the afternoon, when he takes her to 20,000 Leagues. In between, they go to several different diving sites. She's an intermediate scuba diver. He says she's good."

Andrew's elation had him pacing the floor. "Does he know her diving schedule for tomorrow?"

"Yes. If the weather holds, she's going with a group to The Buoy, and in that case she won't be practicing at Thunderball."

He frowned. "Isn't The Buoy infested with sharks?" The thought of what one bite of those jaws could do to her made him shudder.

"That's the whole idea, but it's safe enough. Nobody's lost a limb yet."

On impulse he asked, "Could I dive with them?"

"Look. Don't get me wrong, Governor. You're doing fine, but you're still a novice and you ought to have at least a year's experience before you attempt a dive like that."

"You're right. So where do you suggest we go tomorrow?"

"The Porpoise Pens. It's a ninety-foot dive with black coral and oversize sponges. You'll like it. And there's The Runway—it's got stingrays with eight-foot wingspans."

"Sounds terrific. And around five Randy and I will want to dive at 20,000 Leagues again."

"Naturally," the other man responded with good-natured humor.

"How did you get the information without letting on I was the interested party?"

"That wasn't hard. Since my divorce I've been dating a lot of women and Don knows it. He assumed I'd seen her someplace and was asking for myself, or he never would have said a word. He has his business reputation to think about, too. But we help each other out once in a while, if you get the picture."

"I get it, and I'm very grateful. You've done me a big favor and I won't forget. Thanks, Pokey."

"I'm happy to oblige and I'll see you at the dock at nine as usual."

"We'll be there."

Andrew hung up. So, his mermaid now had a name and a partial address in California—but he wanted to know more. This was a job for his private investigator, Bud Atkins. Casting a glance at Randy, who was singing along with the movie, completely engrossed, Andrew picked up the receiver again.

CHAPTER THREE

LINDSAY HALF LAY in the bottom of the dive boat, the late-afternoon sun shining in her eyes as she struggled into the mermaid costume she wore when she trained here. Wearing panty hose over the bottom half of her bikini helped her ease the stubborn Lycra bodysuit up her legs and hips. Then, holding her breath, she was able to close the side zipper at her waist.

"Being a mermaid isn't all it's chalked up to be," she grumbled in frustration when she saw Don and Ken grinning at her. They were brothers who ran one of the dive shops. "I'd like to see you try it."

"No, no. We're perfectly happy to sit here and watch you, aren't we, Ken?" the middle-aged, balding dive master interjected. "Let me know when you're ready to be tossed overboard."

"I just have to undo my braid." She loosened her hair which hung to below her waist when she stood. "I'm sorry you have to hoist me around like a dead tuna. I feel so foolish and helpless."

"That's no way for a mermaid to talk." Ken, who drove the boat and was a couple of years younger than his brother, winked at her. "We wouldn't miss this chance for the world, would we, Don?"

"Not on your life," Don agreed, scooping Lindsay in his arms as if she were weightless. "I've got me one hunk of half woman here."

"Oh, stop it!" Lindsay laughed softly, but her smile faded when she saw another dive boat in their general vicinity. "Don, isn't that the same boat that was here yesterday?"

"From this distance most of them look alike. What do you think, Ken?"

"Beats me. That diver who took your picture yesterday didn't bother you, did he?"

She shook her head. "Not really. This may sound silly, but I felt like my privacy had been invaded."

Both men burst into laughter. Don said, "Honey, pretty soon your picture is going to be on national television. You can't get much more public than that."

"I know, but—" she shrugged "—I'm still just practicing and . . . I guess it was the shock. I thought I was alone until he showed up. Besides, I was embarrassed—my real costume is a lot less revealing than this." She gestured at the waist-high fish tail and bikini top.

"So what's wrong with giving that diver a heart attack?" Ken guffawed as he lowered an air hose attached to a compressor into the water. It was long enough to reach the ocean floor, so she could easily grab hold of it when she needed air. "He came down here for thrills and you gave him one. He'll probably go home and show it to all his friends. Then when he sees you on TV he can brag that he saw you training."

"It'll be good for business," Don chimed in. "Pretty soon we'll have divers from all over coming to look at the exotic mermaid."

"You two are impossible," she said, but with a smile. "Okay. I'm ready."

"Remember to swim between the colored pennants under the water, and I want you to surface every six minutes without fail. Come up the second you feel too tired."

"I will."

As he lowered her into a dive position, she could hear the sound of the compressor and took a deep breath before plunging into the clear gentle water. Using the dolphin kick, she quickly reached the twenty-foot level, then began the long rolling body motions the choreographer had taught her; they made her hair billow out like a fan, true mermaid-style.

The maneuver was getting easier with practice, but she still had problems when the channels narrowed, so she tried to stay in the wider ones. The colored pennants helped her keep her bearings, and she could tell without looking at her watch when it was time to head for the air hose, which led directly to the boat overhead.

After getting a fresh air supply, she started practicing the technique of gliding, then rising quickly in a graceful arc and turning backward like a ferris wheel, making a complete circle. She spent extra time working on her hand movements, synchronizing them with her body movements.

Throughout the exhausting routine she had to smile and keep her eyes open. At first she found it hard to concentrate, with so many tropical fish providing distractions. But she'd learned to discipline herself. It was important that the routine go as smoothly as possible when the commercial was being shot.

At five and a half minutes into her dive, she rose to the surface, gave Don the OK signal and went down again. But as she executed another circular maneuver, she caught sight of a scuba diver watching her from probably thirty feet away.

He didn't have a camera, but his tall, well-built body and blond hair looked familiar, as did the black-and-pink wet suit. *It was the same man who had filmed her yesterday* Her heart began to race.

No matter what Ken and Don said, she was irritated to think the diver had come back purposely, even if he didn't have his camera this time. She swam for the air hose and could tell he was following her at a discreet distance.

As soon as she'd inhaled enough, she shot off through a narrow gully, thinking he wouldn't be able to twist his way in. But when she looked back, he was still in pursuit. She couldn't see his face hidden behind the mask, and that made him seem more sinister. Lindsay felt as if he was stalking her like the sharks she'd seen earlier in the day, and with the same relentless precision.

What did he want?

She'd heard too many stories from movie stars at the club—and, of course, from Beth's mother—about fanatic admirers who wouldn't leave their idols alone; she couldn't afford to ignore this diver's interest. Using the dolphin kick, she began to propel herself toward the surface to get away from him. To her horror, she couldn't move!

When she looked down she could see that her tail fin had caught in a crisscross of fishing lines—one of the biggest dangers facing a diver—and she felt the first stirrings of panic.

In forty-five seconds she would need more air, yet no matter which way she twisted and tugged, the fin wouldn't come loose. And the boat was no longer above her head, so Don couldn't tell she was in trouble. In her rush to get away, she'd swum beyond the pennants.

Acting on the sheer instinct to survive, she reached for the zipper and yanked at it. That way, she'd be able to slip out of her costume. But the zipper got caught in the material and wouldn't budge.

It was like every story she'd ever heard about survivors of near-drownings—her life started to flash before her. She could hear her parents begging her not to go to the Bahamas, not to take the job. She clawed at the material hugging her waist, but it was no use. She couldn't get it off. Suddenly the diver swam boldly up to her, frightening her so badly she was on the verge of passing out.

In the next instant, strong sure hands pushed hers away and ripped the costume halfway down its side seam, allowing her legs to escape their confinement. She lunged for the surface and when she felt her face break the water, she thankfully drank in huge gulps of air.

The boat was immediately at her side and Don plucked her from the water. "What happened?" He wrapped a fluffy beach towel around her shivering body. "Where's your costume? How come you swam beyond the pennants?"

"I'll tell you as soon as I catch my breath. Please—" she turned to Ken "—I don't want to stay here. Take me back to the hotel now."

"Sure."

Don brought up the air hose while Ken revved the motor, and they took off at top speed for the harbor. Lindsay refused to look back. Though the scuba diver had freed her from a death trap, there was something unnerving about the way he'd lain in wait for her, and she never wanted to see him again.

"Can you talk about it now?" Don asked in a kind voice.

Letting out a shuddering breath, she told him everything that had happened from the moment she first saw the diver until he'd freed her from the costume.

"It sounds like the man saved your life."

Anger provoked her to say, "If he hadn't been down there following me, I would never have run into that fishing line."

"Honey, I'm sorry he scared you. But a fishing line is something we never see until it's too late. It wasn't his fault or yours that your fin got tangled," he said reasonably. "Let's be thankful he returned today to watch you practice, or you might have gotten into some real trouble before I reached you."

While they pulled up to the dock, Lindsay braided her hair and removed her panty hose so she'd look like any normal swimmer when she got out of the boat.

"As soon as we drop you off, we'll go back to the diving site and get your suit. I'm sure it can be repaired in time for tomorrow's practice."

"Thanks, Don. Don't forget to include the extra time when you turn in your hours. And just so you know, until we start filming on Monday I'm not going back to 20,000 Leagues. I can do my practicing at Thunderball. Contrary to what I said earlier, I'd like you in the water with me at all times to keep away any more psychopaths."

"Of course. But isn't 'psychopath' a little strong? The guy problably just wanted to get a good look at you," Don said in a reassuring tone. "You're a beautiful woman, Lindsay. A man would have to be blind not to be interested."

"Thank you for the compliment. But this man was different somehow. He's strong and powerful, and his actions seemed...premeditated, if that makes sense—Oh, I don't know!"

She buried her face in her hands. The image of the blond diver, the way he'd taken charge and dealt with the very crisis he'd precipitated, came forcefully to mind and she shivered.

"I don't like the idea that he has me on videotape. My best friend's mother is an actress who was once stalked by a male fan. It was a horrible time for her and her family."

Don nodded. "Tell you what. When you dive tomorrow, I'll be in the water with you. If Ken or I see anyone in the vicinity matching the man's description, we'll notify harbor security and have him picked up and checked out so you won't have to worry anymore."

Lindsay expelled a sigh of relief. "Thanks, Don. I feel better already."

"It might be a good idea to alert hotel security too," Ken suggested.

"I intend to do that as soon as I get changed," she told him.

"For that matter, we can call around to the other dive shops and find out who took the diver out there. They'll be able to give us a name and an address. If this man is a looney, the police will know where to find him. One wrong move toward you, and you can have him arrested for harassment. They'll confiscate the tape and that'll be the end of it."

"I'll start phoning as soon as we get back," Ken volunteered. "We can't have Lindsay getting nightmares before she becomes a star."

Lindsay smiled at both of them gratefully. "Thank you. For everything."

"We'll call you in a little while."

Substituting a beach robe for the towel, she slipped on her thongs and made her way across the street from the dock to the ultramodern hotel. What she needed was a shower and something icy to drink.

She passed through the lobby to the elevators and hurried to her airy room on the third floor. It was decorated in lemon yellow and cream with bamboo furniture for a cooling yet tropical effect. Sliding doors led to a balcony that faced the harbor and was filled with exotic flowering plants.

Normally Lindsay enjoyed relaxing outside on the lounge chair at the end of the day, never tiring of the soft balmy air and the magical blend of white sand and azure sea. But after her frightening experience, she wouldn't rest until she'd talked to hotel security. She had a premonition the diver would show up again when she least expected it, and she wanted to be prepared.

Lindsay hadn't forgotten that he'd come to her rescue in time to prevent a potentially fatal accident. But anger overrode her gratitude in light of his unwanted, unsolicited attention. She could still feel his hands on her body. She trembled as she recalled the masterful way he'd rid her of the costume. As if he was used to being in authority and to taking charge.

Impatient at her preoccupation with a total stranger, she stepped into the shower and washed her hair. Later, feeling more relaxed, she drank a cola from the mini-bar, then phoned the front desk to speak to the person in charge of security.

When she explained why she was calling, the security supervisor suggested she come down to his office to write out a statement and a description.

Somewhat relieved, she dressed in a sleeveless lilac blouse that brought out the amethyst flecks in her smoky blue eyes. With it, she wore a flowered skirt and the white Italian sandals she preferred, since she didn't need to add height to her five-eight frame.

Except for a pink frost lipstick that enhanced the glow of her Southern California tan, she put on no makeup. Her winged brows and heavy lashes were dark enough on their own. Finally she finished blow-drying her hair until it fell in satiny waves, shimmering like a curtain of gold.

At least once a year since her teens, she'd threatened to cut her hair because it took so much time and work. But something always held her back—probably the fact that it was the one physical attribute that made her feel totally feminine. Now she was thankful she hadn't acted on those impulses: otherwise she wouldn't have been picked for the commercial.

As soon as she was ready, she put the room key in her bag and started for the door, but before she could open it the phone rang. She dismissed the possibility that it was Ken or Don; they wouldn't have had time to return from the dive site or close up the shop yet. Deciding it must be her parents, because they'd called every day since her arrival, she hurried over to the bedside table to answer it. "Hello?"

"Ms. Marshall? This is Leanne at the front desk. Sorry to disturb you, but there's a gentleman down here in the lobby asking to see you. He says he has something of yours. Do you want me to put him through on one of the house phones?"

Lindsay's heart began to hammer with anxiety. "W-will you describe him to me without letting him know what you're doing?" she asked in a shaking voice.

"Right." The receptionist cleared her throat and in hushed tones said, "He's one of the best-looking men I've ever seen. Kind of reminds me of Robert Redford. Midthirties I'd say. Over six feet, blond, hazel eyes, wearing a light gray suit and open-necked shirt."

Lindsay moistened her lips. "Did he tell you his name?"

"No. When I asked, he smiled and said his name wasn't important, but that you'd know who he was."

By now perspiration beaded Lindsay's brow. *How had he found out where she was staying?* She took a shuddering breath. "Leanne, listen carefully. This man has been following me around, bothering me. I've already alerted hotel security about him, and I'm on my way to their office right now. When we get off the phone, act as natural as you can and tell him I'll be down shortly. Anything to detain him. I know—" she gripped the receiver tightly "—ask him to wait out on the garden patio opposite the foyer. Tell him I'll join him for drinks."

There was a long pause. "All right." Another silence followed. "Do you think he's dangerous?"

"I don't know. That's what security is going to find out. Can you get off the phone and pretend everything's okay? I'm depending on you not to arouse his suspicions. I want him stopped right now before this thing goes any further."

"I'll do my best, but I'm nervous."

"I am, too. Just remember that hotel security will be handling this."

The second they said goodbye, Lindsay phoned the number the security man had given her and told him about the latest development. He instructed Lindsay to meet him in the security chief's suite as soon as she could.

Lindsay hung up the phone, dashed from the room and used the stairs to reach the reception room of the chief's office. "Come in, Ms. Marshall." Mr. Herrera greeted her with a handshake and an admiring glance, then asked her to be seated. Lindsay sat in the chair he indicated, trying to remain calm.

"This is a police matter, so I've already taken the liberty of asking one of the waiters to inform this man that you might be detained a few minutes. That should buy us enough time for the officers to get here."

"But what if he leaves before they come?"

"I'll go down to the patio to keep an eye on him, but I can't hold him on mere suspicion. The plan is, when the police arrive I'll point him out and they'll approach him. They'll escort him to the office behind the front desk, where they'll make a few calls, check his identity. It won't take long to find out if there're any warrants out for him. They'll ask him some questions and get a statement as to what he was doing at the dive site waiting for you, following you around."

Lindsay jumped to her feet, too agitated to stay seated. "I'd hate for him to get away before they can do that. My best friend's mother, who's an actress, could never catch the man who stalked her. That's what was so horrible."

"I urged the police to get here quickly. This man, whoever he is, probably just wanted to see you—you're a beautiful woman, Ms. Marshall. But we can't dismiss the possibility that he might have emotional problems, even if he did come to your rescue. So, while you wait here and write up a statement for the police, I'll go downstairs to look into the situation. Don't leave the room until I come back."

She shook her head. "No. I won't. Thank you for your help."

"That's what I'm here for." He disappeared, shutting the door behind him.

He'd left the form on the secretary's desk. Lindsay sat down to write, hardly able to put her thoughts on paper with any coherence because of what she imagined might be going on downstairs.

She stared at the paper without seeing it. She wondered if any of the men she'd been with today really believed the nameless diver constituted a threat to her. Were they simply going through the motions to appease her fears? A man, no matter how sympathetic, would never be able to understand a woman's feelings of vulnerability.

Ken and Don couldn't know how it felt to be watched and followed by a mysterious scuba diver whose powerful build would intimidate most men, let alone Lindsay. Not only was she unfamiliar with the waters, she was virtually helpless in that revealing mermaid costume. She'd carried no protection, not even scuba gear.

It angered her that most men seemed to think a woman's beauty was a justifiable excuse for a man to inflict his attention whenever he felt like it, no matter how unwanted or inappropriate.

Then again, maybe the diver was a would-be actor like Nate, the lifeguard at the Bel Air Club. Perhaps he'd hoped to get friendly with her so he could be introduced to the director of the commercial she was making. The woman at the desk had said he reminded her of Robert Redford.

If that was true, he'd no doubt been told the same thing by countless women; like so many other Hollywood hopefuls, he could be waiting for his big break. Such an absurd scenario was the only one she could halfway understand or excuse. In a way, she hoped that *was* the situation because it meant the man was a nuisance, not a menace.

Half an hour went by. Then another. Lindsay had long since filled out the report and had started pacing the floor. More than once she had to suppress the urge to call the desk to find out if the receptionist knew anything. Her nerves were ragged with anxiety.

Finally the door opened and Mr. Herrera walked in. Right away Lindsay noticed a difference in his demeanor. His dark eyes sparkled, animating his whole face.

She took a step closer, intrigued in spite of the situation. "What happened?"

"A lot more than anyone bargained for." He laughed gently as if entertaining a private joke. "I'm sorry if I sound cryptic, Ms. Marshall. It seems there's been a serious misunderstanding. However, I assure you that you have nothing more to worry about. If you'll come with me to reception, the investigating officer will answer all your questions. Bring the report you filled out with you."

The relief of knowing there was a rational explanation for the diver's behavior put a spring in Lindsay's step as she accompanied the chief of security. The three people in reception, including Leanne, smiled at her with the same expression Mr. Herrera had worn. Something had amused them, and Lindsay felt slightly uncomfortable.

He opened the door behind the counter. "After you, Ms. Marshall."

Her step faltered when she passed over the threshold of the small room and discovered five men in attendance, two in police uniform. Everyone's attention focused on her, but her gaze was drawn to the man whose hazel eyes were assessing her with the same concentration she was giving him.

When she realized what she was doing, she looked away, troubled not only by the intimate eye contact, but by his vague familiarity. This was obviously the culprit, the diver who'd followed her. Now that she could see his face, she realized she'd seen him somewhere before but couldn't remember where or when.

It had nothing to do with his slight resemblance to Robert Redford, either.

Attractive didn't begin to describe him adequately. He was nothing like the lifeguard type she'd originally imagined. And except for his short dark blond hair, its tips bleached by the sun, she could see little else that reminded her of the famous actor.

He was sunburned rather than tanned, attesting to the fact that he didn't regularly spend hours at a beach. His hard-boned features and straight nose lent him a rugged masculinity that matched his tall, powerful physique. He wore an expensive-looking gray suit, just as Leanne had described.

While the others stood around the room, he lounged against the wall, arms folded across his chest, watching her in a way that made her feel uncharacteristically self-conscious.

"Ms. Marshall," one of the policemen said "I'm Officer Ortiz. This is my partner, Officer Henderson. May I have your statement, please?"

Lindsay handed it to him and he studied it briefly, then raised his head. "You say you were afraid that this gentleman—" he glanced at the diver "—intentionally lay in wait for you this afternoon. You suspected him of planning to follow you and harass you. It says here you blame him for the accident that trapped you under the water because you were trying to get away from him. Is that correct?"

Put like that, it made her sound like a foolish alarmist, and she avoided looking at the diver. Taking a deep breath, she said, "Yes. I came to that conclusion after he'd seen me practicing the day before and videotaped me."

By now the man in question had straightened to his full height, and she glimpsed a tiny smile on his lips. It made her blush in remembrance of the moment because what she'd worn had left little to the imagination.

"Yet you admit that when your...mermaid tail became trapped in the fishing line, he swam to your rescue and helped you get out of your costume so you could surface."

"Yes. I give him credit for that. But the point is, I never would have been in that predicament if he'd chosen another diving site to...indulge his interests." She flashed the diver a resentful glance, which he returned with an almost amused gleam in his eyes.

"But he didn't know you'd be practicing there again, and these waters are free to everyone."

Bristling with indignation, she said, "That may be true, but when he saw me, he started following me, instead of leaving me alone. You have to understand what was going on in my mind at the time. For all I knew, he intended to attack me. The mask hid his face and expression. Maybe it was irrational of me to assume the worst, but under the circumstances I felt totally helpless. The dive master didn't know I was in trouble and I was running out of air."

The other two tough-looking men, dressed in shirts and Bermuda shorts much like Mr. Herrera, tried to suppress smiles, and their reaction provoked her anger. She wondered why they were part of the investigation—unless they were undercover agents working with the police.

"It may be impossible for you *gentlemen* to believe, but not all women enjoy a strange man's uninvited attention. If there is a logical reason for why he did what he did, I'd like to hear it. I assume he wants an introduction to the director, but if that's the case, he's gone about it the wrong way. I have no influence whatsoever.'' Her comments brought another smile to everyone's lips, infuriating her even more.

Officer Ortiz tipped his hat. ''Ms. Marshall? The rest of us will wait outside while Governor Cordell explains his side of the story.''

Lindsay blinked. Cordell. Cordell. She searched her memory and then something clicked. Not *Andrew* Cordell, governor of the state of Nevada?

Her gaze lifted to his, and suddenly she knew why she thought she'd seen him before. The ground seemed to give way, and she clutched the edge of the desk to keep her balance.

CHAPTER FOUR

THE MAN SCRUTINIZING her reaction was no longer smiling. "Shall we sit down?" he suggested in a businesslike tone.

"I'd prefer to stand if you don't mind." No matter who he was, he'd given her a real scare. All she wanted was to hear his explanation before she put the whole incident behind her.

The hotel guard and the police obviously held him in awe, but Lindsay had lived around movie stars and celebrities all her life. They were normal men and women, with the usual flaws and virtues, who just happened to make their living in front of millions of people. Governor Cordell was no different, except that he'd caused her one of the most unpleasant moments she'd ever experienced. She wondered what kind of excuse he would proffer.

He made no move to sit. Instead, he studied her taut features for a long moment. "Your instincts were right about me, Ms. Marshall. I did follow you."

His admission jolted her, and her heart began its ridiculous hammering again.

"Worse, I lied to the officer."

She'd never heard anyone less repentant. Her eyes narrowed. "You mean you knew I'd be there again this afternoon to practice my routine?"

"That's right. I made inquiries and deliberately arranged my schedule so I could watch."

At this point she thought maybe she preferred bald-faced lies to this brutal honesty. "Don't tell me. It's difficult to be a peeping Tom when you're a governor, so you've had to resort to getting your thrills underwater."

The full-blown laughter that erupted from him disarmed her completely, even to bringing a reluctant smile to her lips. "I'm sorry. That was rude of me. Mr. Herrera assured me I had nothing to fear from you, but I still haven't heard your explanation."

The laughter faded and his expression sobered. His gaze played over her features with an intimacy that made her want to run away. "That's the problem. I don't have one."

Incredulous, she looked at the floor, unable to sustain his frank appraisal. "Please don't play games with me."

"This is no game, Ms. Marshall." His voice took on a hard quality that reminded her of the authority and decisiveness she'd momentarily experienced. "The honest truth is, I came across a mermaid yesterday and she . . . enchanted me."

Lindsay's eyes lifted to his once more.

"I was so besotted I raced after her, hoping to touch her—just to see if she was real. I've always been told mermaids don't exist, but I have her picture on videotape to prove this one does." He gave Lindsay a rueful smile. "I came back to the same place today to relive the enchantment, never suspecting that my presence would frighten her. When I saw her struggling to free her tail, the enchantment turned to heart-stopping terror and I did what I had to do to allow her to reach the surface. In the process, I damaged her tail, which was left behind.

"Since I know a mermaid has great need of her tail, I brought it to her, hoping she wouldn't be too angry with a mere mortal who unwittingly trespassed in her world—and for a brief moment, lived out his own private fantasy."

"Ms. Marshall?" Officer Ortiz picked that moment to open the door. "We've got another call to respond to. If you've resolved your difficulty, I'll write it up and take my report to the station. If not, Mr. Herrera will carry on until we can come back."

Lindsay had to give the officer credit for doing his job when she was sure he believed she'd wasted his time.

As for Governor Cordell, the honesty of his confession had caught her off guard and left her so confused she no longer knew how she felt about him or the incident. "I-I've been given an explanation I can live with," she admitted in a quiet voice. "Thank you for coming, Officer. I appreciate it very much."

"Our pleasure, Ms. Marshall. Governor." He tipped his hat to both of them. "You two have a nice stay in Nassau."

Once the door closed, the room became claustrophobic. The governor's dominating presence made her feel threatened in new ways she didn't even want to acknowledge.

"You're still frightened of me." He seemed to read her mind with uncanny perception. "Why did you immediately jump to the conclusion there was something sinister in my wanting to watch you perform your routine again? I've heard the explanation you gave the police, but I want to understand the motivation behind it."

His ability to cut straight to the heart of the problem left her stunned. It took Lindsay a few moments to respond. She rested her hip against the edge of the desk, starting to feel the effects of the day's ordeal. Plus, she was weak from hunger because she'd had no food since lunch, which had consisted of only a seafood salad. The mermaid costume for the actual shooting of the commercial had been sewn in one piece from neck to tail and to fit her exact dimensions. It couldn't be enlarged if she gained weight.

"I assume you've seen films starring Victoria Harris?" she began. He gave a brief nod, seeming to concentrate on her mouth as she spoke, disrupting her train of thought.

"Her daughter, Beth, and I have been best friends since kindergarten. Our parents' backyards face each other. We grew up as close as sisters, and because we were both only children, it was natural that we practically lived at each other's houses. Vicky's like an aunt to me, and though her marriages haven't worked out, she's really a wonderful person and I adore her."

Lindsay could hear the tremor in her voice. Tears came to her eyes when she recalled the older woman's kindness and encouragement during those difficult years while she was learning to walk again. Embarrassed to have revealed so much in front of this man who was little more than a stranger, Lindsay wiped the moisture from her lashes.

"I'm indebted to her for many things, including the opportunity to make this commercial. She's a very kind and giving person. She's also one of the most beautiful women in the world. About ten years ago—while she was doing a benefit to help raise funds for a children's charity—an attractive man from the audience went backstage to take her picture. Then he sent a copy of it to her house. He enclosed a love letter with the photo."

Lindsay still remembered the incident vividly. "Vicky was shocked because she couldn't imagine how he'd gotten her address. And the personal things written in the letter made her feel ill. Vicky's husband at the time, Pat—an alcoholic—told her not to worry about it.

"A month later another envelope arrived with a letter and more pictures, this time showing her coming out of a store on Wilshire Boulevard with Beth. It meant he'd been following her everywhere. That's when the nightmare really began and the police were called in." The horror of it had haunted Lindsay for a long time after.

"Vicky hired bodyguards who came to live on the grounds and accompanied her and Beth whenever they left the house. During that period my parents wouldn't allow me to associate with Beth at all." Lindsay's voice shook with remembered pain. "That's why—"

"You don't need to explain further," he broke in, and she lifted her head to discover a self-denigrating grimace on his face. "Did the police catch the man responsible for terrorizing them?"

She shook her head. "No. The pattern continued for a full year without a lead. Then one day, the letters and pictures stopped coming. Needless to say, Beth and Vicky's lives were changed forever by what had happened. Pat couldn't handle the pressure and walked out on her at a time when she needed his support. He might have been the wrong man for her, but naturally she was devastated that her third marriage had failed, and she began looking for another anchor.

"Beth needed a lot of therapy, so I didn't see as much of her anymore, and my parents were still wary of any contact. In a sense, my life was irrevocably changed, as well, because—" she paused "—because I suppose it brought an end to my innocence."

The silence in the tiny room exacerbated Lindsay's feelings of discomfort. How had Andrew Cordell managed to elicit such a response when a half hour ago she had regarded him as a villain and had been ready to press charges?

Needing to escape the confines of the room and his disturbing proximity, she said, "I'm sorry to have turned this into a major incident. Don, my dive master, said divers occasionally get caught in fishing lines and that I'd probably have run into it whether you were there or not."

Unable to help herself, she lifted troubled eyes to him. "Thank you for coming to my rescue. Your quick thinking probably saved my life."

His expression grew bleak. "You were right before. My presence frightened you and broke your concentration. After what you've told me, I wouldn't blame you if you shot the next suspicious-acting male on sight. I take full blame for the entire incident. Even though I'd like to excuse myself on the grounds that I was under a mermaid's spell at the time, I can't do that."

She could tell he was genuinely sorry for arousing such fear in her, and his comment—combined with the irresistible charm that broke through her defenses—brought the first real smile to her lips. "I can't believe I'm saying this, but I think I'm flattered by the compliment. Maybe it means my commercial will be convincing enough, after all. Do you have any idea how difficult it is to imitate a fish?"

"I think I do," he murmured. "Once you'd left, I cut the fishing lines to free your tail, I took it back to the house to see what I could do about getting it repaired. When Randy and I examined it, neither of us could figure out how you get into it, let alone how you manage to do all those maneuvers. It must feel like a vise! Obviously you're an exceptionally talented swimmer."

"Let's just say I've had a lot of practice," she responded, warming to him for being considerate enough to salvage her costume. Don and Ken would have made a wasted trip back to the dive site to get it. "Is Randy the dive master?"

A wry smile broke the corner of his mouth, drawing her attention to the laugh lines radiating from either side. "Randy is my eighteen-year-old son who's dying to meet you in person."

Everything he said intrigued her, and a growing curiosity about the man overrode her usual caution. "Are you here on a family vacation, then?"

"That's right. It's the first pleasure trip Randy and I have taken together since my wife died three years ago."

Now that he mentioned it, she did remember reading something in the newspaper about his loss. Two years before, when the general election results were published, they'd revealed the histories of the winning western gubernatorial candidates. "That must have been a tragic time for you," she said somberly. "I feel worse than ever that the police had to be called in, disrupting your holiday."

One dark blond eyebrow arched. "Well, I won't pretend that I was overjoyed when two police officers started to approach my table. They surprised the hell out of me and my bodyguards, who intercepted them and demanded they state their business. I have to admit I was shocked when they asked me to step behind the desk because they wanted to ask me a few questions regarding a certain mermaid."

Lindsay tried to keep a straight face, but a gentle laugh escaped, anyway.

"This gets worse." The mirth in his eyes was contagious. "Some reporter must have picked up the hotel security guard's call over the police band, because a flashbulb went off as I walked through the foyer carrying your mermaid costume in my arms. For the most part it was camouflaged—except for the tail fin."

"You're not serious!" Lindsay cried in dismay.

"I'm afraid I am, and the newspapers will turn this into a scandal I'll probably never live down." But he said it with a lopsided smile. "I had the costume delivered to your room, by the way."

She groaned in disbelief, knowing better than most people that a prominent man like the governor had to deal with gross distortions and sensationalism from the media every time he turned around. If she'd truly been his enemy, she couldn't have picked a better way to diminish him, not only in front of his loyal constituents, but the voters who'd opposed him at the polls. "I'm so sorry."

"Don't be," he muttered. "I'm the one who created this predicament. It's you I'm concerned about—more so now that you've given me an opportunity to understand your fears. Just so you know, while I was waiting for Mr. Herrera to bring you down, I instructed my people to take the necessary measures to prevent your name from being published, but I can't guarantee anything."

"I appreciate that," Lindsay murmured, starting to reel as she considered all the ramifications. *If her parents heard about this . . .*

"For your protection against any more curious mortals who might fall under your enchantment, you'll be leaving this room with two armed guards. They'll be on hand day and night throughout the rest of your stay in Nassau and will escort you back to California."

"Surely that's not necessary!"

"I'm afraid it is. Once the incident is public knowledge, and it will be within a matter of hours, every crackpot around will come out of the woodwork to get a look at you—or worse. When that happens you'll be glad of the protection."

She believed him and felt like a fool. "Does this mean I'll be depriving you of your bodyguards?"

"No. I always travel with security personnel and can spare a couple of men to guard you. But they'll be working at *my* expense, not the taxpayer's. In case you're wondering."

He really did have the unnerving ability to read her mind, and a dark red blush deepened the tan on her face and neck. He also knew things about her she hadn't told him. "How did you find out I live in California?"

His quick smile made him look younger and more carefree. "I was hoping you wouldn't ask. I may have many sins, but lying isn't one of them. I admit I paid someone a little extra to do undercover work for me. I found my dive master, Pokey, a terrific resource, since he's good friends with your dive master, Don."

Her thoughts darted back to various conversations she'd had with Don and his brother, Ken. *How much had they told him about her, and how come Don had never mentioned a word?*

"Before you get angry with Don, I should assure you that he had no idea Pokey was inquiring on my behalf. He let your dive master assume he was asking questions because of his own curiosity." There was a slight pause while he observed her reaction. "I'm unscrupulous, I know, and my political opponents never let me or the voting public forget it once the campaigning starts."

He was outrageous and arrogant and overconfident, yet those very traits somehow heightened his appeal. Lindsay was so spellbound by his intelligence and charismatic personality, she'd forgotten everything else, including how hungry she was. When she glanced at her watch, she noticed it was after nine. They'd been talking for over an hour! "It's gotten late. I have to go."

He nodded. "I should have been back to take Randy to dinner at least two hours ago. Give me five minutes to leave the hotel first, then feel free to do whatever you want. With luck, my departure will draw attention away from you."

"Thank you," she whispered, strangely moved by his consideration, yet somewhat deflated that she wouldn't be seeing him again—which made no sense at all.

"One more thing, Ms. Marshall." He leaned negligently against the door, hands in his pockets, allowing her a glimpse of his hard-muscled physique, the way the material of his suit molded his powerful thighs. "If you want the video, I'll have it delivered to your room."

She smoothed the hair away from her cheek. He had done everything humanly possibly to reduce her fears, and she admired him for that kind of concern. "That won't be necessary. I trust you to be discreet. Besides, most videos end up in a closet or cupboard and never see the light of day again."

"Don't count on it," he warned, staring at her through narrowed eyes. Then he opened the door and was gone.

Lindsay stood there in a daze, aware that something vital had gone out of the room—and maybe her life.

After the agreed-upon five minutes, she started to walk out the door and was confronted by the hotel security chief and two fit-looking men in their midthirties.

"I take it all is well?"

"Yes, thank you, Mr. Herrera," she murmured. "I'm very grateful to you for helping me with my problem, even though it turned out to be a harmless incident, after all."

"I'm glad it had a happy ending. Lets you enjoy the rest of your visit. Now, let me introduce you to Mr. Garvey and Mr. Arce, the men Governor Cordell has assigned to protect you."

"Jake and Fernando will do." The two men, who were dressed like typical American tourists, shook hands with her and were very cordial, but Lindsay still felt a sense of unreality about the entire situation.

"The governor told us you weren't too happy about needing protection," Fernando said, "but any story coming out in the paper will put you at risk. You'll be thankful the governor took precautions, because you never know how the public will react, especially the local groupies."

"That's right," Jake added. "The governor feels responsible for implicating you in the first place, and take my word for it, he won't rest unless he knows you're safe. Don't ever tell him we told you this, but around the governor's mansion he's known as the worrywart. His wife used to call him that, and it stuck."

Lindsay chuckled at this unexpected insight into an endearing facet of his character. She couldn't imagine a man who looked or acted less like a worrywart than Governor Cordell.

"For security reasons, the governor's had your room changed to the penthouse suite. A private elevator leads up from the garage. We'll be staying in adjoining rooms to ensure your privacy and safety."

The governor moved with a speed that took her breath away. But she couldn't possibly accept such a gesture. "Please convey my thanks, but I'll stay in the room I have now ."

"I'm afraid it's too late, Ms. Marshall. Your things have already been moved to the suite and your old room readied for another guest. Shall we go?"

"I'll show you to the private elevator," Mr. Herrera offered.

Bemused by her change in circumstances, Lindsay could only nod and follow him out to the foyer. She ignored the interested stares of the employees in reception.

Fernando stayed close by while Jake sauntered off. She assumed he'd gone on ahead to scout the premises. Lindsay knew how they worked because of Beth and Vicky's experience.

Little did she dream when she'd first called Mr. Herrera for help that the sinister-seeming diver would turn out to be her protector instead of her tormentor. One word from him had turned Lindsay's world upside down, changing it into a new and unfamiliar one, complete with personal bodyguards and plush new surroundings.

The man had gone to great lengths to make up for any pain or inconvenience he'd caused her. His efforts revealed a far more generous nature than she would have credited him with when she'd first met him.

The first thing Lindsay noticed when the elevator door opened to her new lodgings was an entry hall with doors leading off on both sides. Beyond it was a gray-and-white living room with matching white silk moiré couches facing each other around a huge glass coffee table. She could see her mermaid costume incongruously stretched out on one of the couches.

The walls of this elegant suite were hung with modern art, a black baby-grand piano sat at one end, and a fabulous Chinese screen stood at the other. It partially hid a teak dining room table and chairs for ten.

Potted trees and flowering plants were attractively arranged against the plantation shutters running the length of the room. On opposite walls at either end were sets of French doors leading to the other parts of the suite.

Fernando gave Lindsay a tour, showing her the breakfast room and kitchen, and a sitting room and bathroom off the master bedroom.

She followed him across the pearl gray carpeting, enjoying the feel of the deep pile. When he opened the shutters in front of the sliding glass doors, she could see the walk-out patio with its umbrella table, lounge chairs and more flowering plants silhouetted against the night sky. The perfumed air mingling with the scent of the sea felt soft against her skin.

"Everything is in order, Ms. Marshall. Let me know if you plan to leave the hotel."

"I don't. I'm going to eat and go to bed. I'll be up and ready to leave for the harbor by six-fifteen."

He nodded. "We've already been in contact with your dive master and apprised him of the new setup. The governor ordered your dinner before he left, and all I have to do is call the kitchen. When they bring it up, I'll put it on the breakfast room table. Do you need anything else?"

Lindsay looked around. "No. Everything's perfect. You've made me feel like a princess."

He smiled. "The governor told us to treat you like one. And believe me, from where I'm standing, it isn't that hard. Forgive me for saying something so unprofessional, but I've never seen hair that beautiful."

"Most of the time it's a complete nuisance, but thank you for the compliment, Fernando."

"Anytime." He smiled. "After I've served your dinner, I'll be in the room to the left of the foyer. Jake will take the right. Any problems, and you can ring our rooms by dialing one-zero or one-one."

"I don't anticipate any, but thanks just the same." She knew there was no point in protesting what seemed to her to be excessive precautions.

"We'll be answering all incoming phone calls. If they're legitimate, we'll put them on hold and ring through to you. Feel free to make any phone calls you like. Just remember that all incoming and outgoing calls will be taped. We'll give you the tape when you get back to California."

An involuntary shiver ran down Lindsay's spine. The governor's power was like a velvet glove that hid a fist of tempered steel.

How did people live like this on a daily basis? Lindsay knew she never could. It reminded her too much of those last few years at home with her overprotective parents; they'd demanded to know her every move and feared something might happen to her with every breath she took.

Trying to shake off the claustrophobic feeling those memories gave her, she hurried into the master suite and got ready for bed. No sooner had she slipped into her nightgown and robe than the phone rang. She assumed it was Jake or Fernando letting her know her dinner had arrived.

"Hello?"

"Ms. Marshall?" a deep familiar voice sounded in her ear, creating a quickening in her body.

"Yes, Governor?"

"Call me Andrew. It helps me forget my responsibilities for a little while."

She hugged the telephone cord to her chest. "Aren't you worried about what your constituents would think if they heard that?" she teased.

His soft chuckle delighted her. "If Jake and Fernando are doing their job, then I don't have any worries."

"They've been wonderful and the suite is lovely." She took a steadying breath to slow her heartbeat. "Thank you for your generosity. But please, don't do anything more. I—I know you're sorry for what happened. But I feel bad because of what I've done to disrupt what should have been a worry-free vacation for you and your son. I'd like to repay you for any inconvenience I've caused you, but I can't. So please, don't make me any more indebted to you than I already am or I'll feel terrible."

"Terrible enough to have dinner with me and Randy tomorrow evening? Come to the house after you're through diving for the day. We've taped all our dives so far—you might get a laugh out of watching two novices blunder their way around the reefs. You might enjoy seeing the film I took of you, too. That is, if you're not busy."

The invitation caught her completely off guard. It also thrilled her, and that in itself was frightening. If she spent any more time in this man's company, she knew instinctively she'd crave more and more.

"Aren't you curious to see what the last surviving mermaid looks like?" he asked in a husky voice. "It's a sight every human should witness at least once before she swims back to sea and disappears forever."

Was this the governor's way of telling her this was just a vacation fling? Nothing more? The thought depressed her and she felt more confused and out of sorts than ever.

Half-seriously she said, "Maybe she disappears because she's not a true mermaid."

"I refuse to believe that," he threw back with an intensity that took her by surprise. "But I'll let you be the judge. Randy and I'll look for you around seven-thirty."

She absently traced the end of the receiver with the tip of her finger. "I'll be practicing until seven, so I can't promise to be there right on the dot."

"I don't care if you don't show up until midnight, as long as you come." At his word, the fervor of his tone, her legs felt as insubstantial as mashed potatoes. "Jake and Fernando know the way. One last thing. If you don't want to be upset tomorrow, don't read the newspapers. All right?"

"All right. Thank you for everything including the dinner invitation. Good night, gov—Andrew."

Her hands were actually trembling as she replaced the receiver. She wanted to blame it on hunger, but she knew differently.

On her way to the breakfast room for her meal she paused to examine her mermaid costume. Someone had sewn the long rip down the side and repaired the zipper.

How had he found a seamstress or a tailor so quickly? Nothing he wanted seemed beyond his reach or control. That was exactly what Lindsay feared....

CHAPTER FIVE

"HEY, DAD? It's Uncle Zack on the line."

Since his brother-in-law would never call him unless there was an emergency, it could only mean one thing. Andrew threw down the front section of the *Los Angeles Examiner* in disgust and went over to pick up the bedside phone.

"Zack? I take it you just saw the newspaper."

"It was kind of hard not to. The headline in the *Sun* reads Governor Cordell Saves Beautiful Mermaid in Heroic Rescue, and there's a big picture of you carrying something that looks suspiciously like a fish tail. For the love of heaven, Andrew, I used to worry about Randy's name showing up in the gossip columns, but *you* made the front page." Zack didn't even try to control his laughter.

Andrew groaned. "Nothing is sacred these days. I was afraid the press would get ahold of the story."

"Alex sends her love and told me to tell you to look on the bright side. She thinks a touch of romance is exactly what the governor's office needs."

Sinking down on the edge of the bed Andrew asked, "And what do *you* think?"

Ever astute, Zack murmured, "For a long time I've been hoping and praying you'd find someone to replace my sister. You're too young and full of life to go on alone. But a *mermaid?*"

Laughter burst out of Andrew, and Zack joined in. It felt good.

"Is she worth the damage to your public image, brother?" came the perceptive question.

Andrew had been asking himself the same thing. His hand tightened on the receiver. "Do you know that when I first saw her, there were a few seconds when I wondered if she really was a mermaid?"

"That beautiful, huh?"

"I have her on videotape and I've replayed it so many times I'm afraid it'll break. I'm beginning to understand your fixation on Alex. Randy says you kept all her posters in your bedroom after telling him you'd destroyed them."

"Jeez, Dad!" Andrew heard Randy grumble in the background.

Zack sounded equally unhappy. "Is nothing in my house private?"

"No. Not in your house or in mine. Thanks to this incident, I've been made out as everything from a drunken, deviant, washed-up civil servant to a lecherous, depraved member of the mob, lying in wait to accost young unsuspecting mermaids."

"And did you? Accost her, I mean."

"What do *you* think?"

"I'm the wrong man to ask. The first time Alex and I were alone together and I took her on a tour of the ranch, I actually told her I'd meet her price if she'd pose on Domino for a picture to help advertise him. I'm still ashamed of how I acted that day."

"Pose in what?"

"Nothing but an overhanging wild-rose tree."

Andrew smiled to himself, shaking his head. "And I thought I knew everything there was to know about Zackery Quinn."

"You don't know the half of it."

"Yes, I think I do, if my experience of the past few days is any barometer," Andrew murmured on a more serious note. "She's ten years younger than I am, Zack."

"So?"

"She's afraid of me."

"What did you do to her?"

Andrew took the next ten minutes to explain everything, including the fact that she was coming to the house for dinner that evening. He left out nothing except his most private and personal thoughts. "One of these days you'll see her on television advertising Beauty from the Sea cosmetics. She'll make the owner of that company a rich man."

"Dad," Randy interrupted, "tell him to put Troy on."

"Zack? Randy wants to talk to Troy."

"He's out with some of the men. I'll tell him to call as soon as he gets in. He's been hoping to talk to Randy."

Andrew conveyed the message to Randy, then returned to their conversation. "I appreciate your call, Zack. It helps keep me sane at a time like this."

"Other than that, how are you enjoying the trip?" Zack asked.

"Randy and I are having the time of our lives."

"That's what I wanted to hear. You're lucky to have a son like him." Andrew could hear a certain wistfulness in Zack's voice.

"Don't you know the sex of your baby yet? These days I thought everybody did."

"No. Alex and I decided we don't want to know. It makes the waiting more fun."

"I agree. Give her my love and tell her not to have it before we get back."

"She's not due till the end of the month."

"Then we'll definitely be home in time. Keep in touch, Zack. If she has the baby early, we want to be the first to congratulate you."

They said goodbye and Andrew hung up. Talking with Zack had lightened his mood considerably. He tossed all the newspapers with their scandalous fallacious reporting in the wastebasket and turned to Randy. "Let's dive the Clifton Wall today."

He made the suggestion because he was counting the hours until he saw Lindsay Marshall again; he thought he'd go crazy if he had to sit around the house all day. He could tell he'd surprised his son, who, like the security guards, assumed they would stay in to avoid the inevitable curiosity seekers.

His eyes lit up. "You mean it?"

"Don't I always?"

"Yeah, but isn't it for experienced divers?"

"I'll bet we can talk Pokey into taking us down to a safe depth. On the way to the dock, let's stop for more videotape. While we're gone the cook can arrange our dinner party."

Randy eyed his father steadily. "I haven't seen you this excited since a long time before Mom died. Ms.

Marshall must not be too mad at you, or she wouldn't be coming here tonight. Just don't do anything to scare her off, Dad."

"What's that supposed to mean?" Andrew asked with a bark of laughter. "Is my son lecturing me on the proper way to treat a lady?"

"Yeah." Randy grinned. "You haven't been with a woman you liked in three years, and seeing your attraction to Ms. Marshall, I just—"

"Thank you, Randy," Andrew interrupted, feeling a tenderness for his son that transformed itself into a bear hug. "It's a good thing you're around to give your old dad sound advice. I'll keep it in mind."

THE GOVERNOR'S VACATION retreat reminded Lindsay of the stark white villas one saw in posters of the Greek Islands. In the twilight, the colorful petals of flowering shrubs and trees among the greenery looked luminescent.

As the limousine rounded a curve leading to the front entry, Lindsay almost told the driver to take her back to the hotel. All day long she'd been anticipating the moment when she saw *him* again. By now, she was filled with so many conflicting emotions she wasn't sure she could go through with it.

In retrospect, she realized she'd overreacted the day before when she'd thought he posed a threat to her. But now that she knew the truth, she felt a different kind of tension.

While she was getting ready, she had changed outfits several times, wondering whether she should dress up or down to please him. Eventually she had decided on a sleeveless, dusky pink sheath in raw silk, with a

Chinese collar and a modest slit up one side. Underneath, she wore a lace-trimmed slip of the same hue and matching low-heeled sling-back pumps.

She'd left her hair loose, and it fell over her right shoulder, exposing one of her earrings, a small pink topaz in a ball-like crystal shape that borrowed light and color from her dress. Like many of her things, they'd been a gift from her parents.

Jake had stayed behind at the hotel while Fernando rode in the back seat of the limo with Lindsay. When the driver had circled the fountain and pulled to a stop, the ever-vigilant Fernando jumped out of the car to assist her.

Immediately the front doors of the villa opened, and Andrew Cordell stood silhouetted in the entry, far too appealing for Lindsay's peace of mind. He drew her gaze like a homing beam. She fastened her avid eyes on his face, his blond hair—more sun-bleached than she remembered—his skin with its newly acquired tan.

Her gaze wandered lower to his elegant summer suit, which hinted seductively at his powerful frame. Its light caramel shade was toned with a darker shirt and contrasting silk tie. Despite his relaxed pose, he radiated a charged vitality, an energy that Lindsay's body sensed even from the distance separating them. On less than steady legs, she walked up the steps toward him.

"I lied when I told you I didn't care what time you got here. It's after eight, and I was about ready to come after you myself." He sounded as if he meant every word, and her mouth went dry from nervous excitement.

"I wanted to be on time, but Ken had trouble getting the boat started after I was through diving."

"I'll try to forgive him," he murmured, clasping her elbow to usher her inside. The doors closed quietly behind them, and for some reason, that gave her the same feeling she'd experienced when she dove a wall whose shelf plunged vertically into deep blue water fathoms below. She'd known she was swimming out of her depth; she knew it now.

She was acutely conscious of the touch of his hand. With all the turmoil she felt at his nearness, Lindsay could scarcely appreciate the beauty of her surroundings.

There was a certain irony in that, she reflected wryly. She'd lived in the film capital of the world all her life. She'd grown up around affluent good-looking men. Her parents had hosted hundreds of parties over the past decade; she'd met producers, movie stars and important dignitaries most women would find exceptionally attractive.

So why, out of all the men of her acquaintance, was Andrew Cordell the one—the *only* one—who could bring her alive with a look or a touch?

He led her around a center atrium containing an assortment of exotic tropical plants and past a sunken living room with Mediterranean-style arched alcove windows facing the sea. On her left, she glimpsed a formal dining room through another alcove.

"My son is waiting for us in the study," Andrew said, guiding her to a room whose lattice walls and furnishings created a Moorish flavor.

When they entered the doorway, an attractive suntanned young man with dark hair got up from a crouched position in front of the entertainment center, a stack of videotapes beside him. He brushed off his slacks and straightened his navy blazer with a charming grin.

"Hi," he said to Lindsay, and she immediately saw Andrew Cordell as he must have looked twenty years before.

"Randy?" His father still held Lindsay's arm in a possessive grip. "Allow me to introduce you to a real live mermaid. Can you believe she goes by the name of Ms. Lindsay Marshall?"

Amused by his comment, she smiled and shook his son's hand. "Hello, Randy. I hope you'll call me Lindsay."

"Does that go for me, too?" her host demanded.

"Of course," she said a little breathlessly. He'd asked the question without an accompanying smile.

"We're glad you came, Lindsay." Randy's comment broke the tension. "When Dad showed me the video of you, I could understand why he thought he'd seen a real mermaid. It's great footage. Wait till you see it!"

"I'm almost afraid to. I had taken in too much air and my body wanted to rise while I was trying to swim on a level plane. My arms were flailing all over the place."

"I'm afraid neither of us noticed your difficulty," Andrew admitted in a low aside before releasing her arm. "Would you like something to drink before we eat dinner?"

"I don't think so. To be honest, I'm always starving after practice."

"We can remedy that in a big hurry." While he spoke, his way of concentrating on her mouth shot another tremor through her already sensitized body. She could still feel the place where his hand had held her.

"I'll tell the cook we're ready."

"Thanks, Randy," Andrew said over his shoulder. "We'll be right there."

"He's a good-looking young man. Except for his coloring, which is a little darker than yours, he resembles you."

"Thank you. However, I think his nicest traits were inherited from his mother."

"Do you have other children?"

"No. We were lucky to have Randy. My wife suffered from a rare blood disease that afflicted her mother, as well. It took both of them early in life."

Lindsay lifted pained eyes to his. "Losing someone you love would be traumatic enough. But to be in the public eye at a time like that must have been dreadful."

His jaw hardened. "It was hell, particularly for Randy. Because of the demands placed on me, he ended up having to cope with a great deal of grief on his own. I'm trying to make up for that now."

She hugged her arms to her waist. "I wish I'd known all this befo—"

"Don't regret anything," he broke in unexpectedly. "I was determined to meet you. The only thing is that the *manner* of our meeting wasn't quite what I had in mind—being introduced under armed guard with the press lurking in the wings. I confess I would have preferred our first meeting to have gone according to my original plan. It certainly would have been less public."

Her heart leapt at his admission. "Your original plan?"

"I was going to wait until you'd finished diving for the day. Pokey and his crew had instructions to bring our boat alongside yours. At that point, he was going to ask Don to introduce us and give me the opportunity to apologize for having strayed into your territory the day before. If you were receptive, I intended to ask you out to dinner so I could give you the videotape if you wanted it."

He paused and stared directly into her eyes. "Would you have accepted my invitation?"

Lindsay had been listening to his explanation with a sense of wonder and was startled by his question. Something told her that no matter how upset she'd been by his almost sinister appearance underwater, his persuasive personality would have won her over. She suspected that same charisma had garnered the votes needed to elect him to a second term of office. If she remembered correctly, he'd achieved a landslide victory.

"Dinner's ready, Dad."

The interruption couldn't have come at a better moment for Lindsay, who was floundering as she searched for a response.

Without taking his eyes off her, Andrew said, "We'll be right there." Again Lindsay felt the warmth of his hand steal through her body. It rested at the back of her waist, urging her forward. Before they reached the dining room he murmured into her hair,

"If your presence here this evening is any indication, then I take it the answer would have been yes."

Hot-faced, she kept on walking and was surprised to discover they were dining on the connecting terrace, which was surrounded by a hedge and flowering shrubbery to assure complete privacy.

The circular table held a centerpiece of exotic orchids illuminated by candlelight. Between the softness of the perfumed night air and the brillant three-quarter moon rising in the velvet sky, Lindsay couldn't quite believe any of this was real. She was suddenly reminded of her conversation with Beth at the airport.

Just twenty-four hours ago she'd been sitting in Mr. Herrera's office, believing that the man now at her side was being arrested for harassment. The whole situation had taken an unexpected 180-degree turn, and she was still dizzy from the effect.

"How come we haven't seen you in any movies?" Randy wanted to know once they'd been served a delicious stuffed-shrimp appetizer by one of the kitchen staff.

Lindsay choked a little on her white wine and put the glass back on the table. "Because I'm not an actress."

"You're so beautiful you must be a model, then." His direct way of speaking was like his father's.

She shook her head and smiled. "Thank you for the lovely compliment, but you're wrong again. I'm working on the commercial to make enough money to go to graduate school this fall. The only reason I was hired for the role of mermaid is that I'm a strong swimmer and I've got long hair."

"Surely not the only one," Andrew muttered, an indecipherable expression darkening his eyes as they wandered over her features. "What are you planning to study, and where?" he asked, revealing the same intensity she'd noticed from the beginning, as if her answer mattered a great deal to him.

"I'm pursuing my master's in marine biology at Scripp's Institute in La Jolla."

"I've heard of that!" Randy interjected. "A couple of my friends attended Sea Camp there last summer."

"That's right. Several of my old friends did the very same thing when they were freshmen in high school. One day I plan to study shark behavior, that kind of thing."

"You're kidding! That's fantastic. Did you see a lot of sharks during your dive yesterday? Dad and I wanted to join you, but we're not in your class of diver yet."

Apparently they knew everything about her daily schedule, thanks to Don, yet Randy didn't act the least abashed about his father's unorthodox method of gathering personal information. She glanced at Andrew, expecting to see a grin, and was surprised by the grimace that crossed his face.

Belatedly she answered Randy's question. "There were eight, as I recall."

By now the main course had arrived—a delectable rack of lamb, potatoes au gratin and glazed carrots. While they ate, she could still feel the tension emanating from her host.

"Surely out of all the fish in the sea, sharks are the most dangerous," Andrew said. "Why would you deliberately choose a career most people consider high-risk?"

She'd been asked that question more times than she cared to remember; in fact, she could still hear the shock in her parents' voices when she'd told them her plans.

Resting her fork on the dinner plate, she said, "There's little risk if you've been educated to deal with sharks and their behavior. Let me ask you a question. What made you go into politics, a career I consider much riskier, not only to your family but to your own physical and emotional health?"

Their eyes held. "You're using the wrong analogy. If the sharks get me, politically speaking, I can always go back to being a district attorney. What choice do you have if a great white decides to make you his next meal?"

She took another sip of wine before responding. "It's true that on very rare occasions a great white has been known to ambush a human, but it isn't the only kind of shark in the ocean. Hammerheads provide a fascinating study for scientists—and their mouths aren't as big."

"So they only take a bite out of you, instead of making you the entire meal, is that what you're saying?"

She sucked in her breath, surprised he hadn't seen the humor in her remark. "Any living creature will become defensive if it's cornered or hurt. A shark is no different in that regard. If studying them was that dangerous, no one would live to tell about it."

"What kinds of things do you do with them?" Randy wanted to know.

Lindsay wiped her mouth with a napkin. "Well, to give you one example, a shark has to be tagged to track its migration habits. So the swimmer has to get close to it to make sure the transmitter is shot into the musculature of its top midsection. Sometimes the initial pain causes the shark to retaliate. Naturally the swimmer is aware of this and takes every precaution to ensure his or her safety."

"Is that what you're going to be doing this fall?" Randy asked, his face shining with interest.

"No. Scripp's offers a six-year program. I'll be doing class work the first year. Then I'll take a stringent diving course for a couple of weeks, and after that I'll start working on some underwater hands-on projects with actual research scientists."

"That sounds like something I'd love to do!" Randy said excitedly.

"Fortunately you have four years of college ahead of you, during which you'll change your mind at least a dozen times," Andrew said sharply before Lindsay could respond. "If everyone's finished, why don't we retire to the study where we can be served dessert and let Lindsay see herself on video?"

"I'm not sure I'm ready for this," she said as Andrew got up to usher her from the table. She sensed undercurrents here and wondered if Randy's interest in scuba diving went deeper than mere pleasure. If so, it might explain his father's desire to change the subject. The possible dangers inherent in underwater activity of any kind, coupled with his wife's death, had probably made Andrew more protective of his only son.

No one understood that better than Lindsay. She couldn't help recalling several conversations she'd had with the psychiatrist about parents like hers who clung to their children because of an underlying fear for their safety. Andrew Cordell fit the mold, and if what she suspected was true, she felt sorry for both father and son.

Randy hurried ahead of them and had chairs waiting in front of the TV when Andrew led her into the study, his hand again at her waist.

Did he treat all women in such a personal way? She wondered how Randy felt about it, or had he long ago accepted the fact that his father was an eligible bachelor who acquired a female escort whenever his high-profile position demanded one?

Except that tonight was anything but high-profile. In fact, he'd done everything in his power to keep her name out of the papers and their acquaintance a secret. So why had he invited her to his vacation home?

There was only one answer that made sense to Lindsay. The governor's overactive conscience had obviously led him to offer a gesture of apology, even though she'd told him she felt guilty for her own part in exposing him to ridicule.

After tonight she would probably never see him or his son again. The thought was so depressing she made up her mind to enjoy this evening to the fullest. On impulse she said, "Before I look at any pictures of me, I'd like to see the other videos you've taken since coming to the Bahamas. Maybe by then I'll be able to handle my less than expert performance." *And* she could legitimately feast her eyes on Andrew Cordell without letting on how strong her attrraction to him had become.

The next hour passed quickly as Lindsay sat mesmerized by the footage. "For a couple of amateurs, you two are terrific divers and the videos are spectacular!" she exclaimed in the darkened room. "How did you learn to operate an underwater camera so well? I'm jealous of all the dives you've made—and documented."

"My friend, Troy, who's kind of related to me now, is great with cameras. He'll probably end up taking pictures for *National Geographic* or some other famous magazine one day. Anyway, he showed us how to work it."

"I'm impressed, Randy. Does he scuba dive, too?"

"No. He broke his leg really badly playing football a couple of years ago and hasn't done any sports since."

"That's too bad," Lindsay mused aloud. "Swimming would be excellent therapy for him."

Randy's head jerked around. "You think so?"

"I know so." She smiled, aware of Andrew's eyes on her. "I teach swimming, and some of my students are handicapped or recovering from accidents, like Troy. For many of them, swimming therapy is essential to their recovery."

"Do you think he could certify for scuba diving?"

"Of course."

"Dad? Did you hear that?"

"I'm way ahead of you, Randy. When we get back home we'll tell him what Lindsay said and maybe he can certify in time to go to the Cayman Islands with us in August."

"I've been told that's a photographer's dream," Lindsay murmured, gazing in fascination at the underwater paradise on the TV screen. Still, despite the beauty of the coral and the colorful fish, she could hardly tear her eyes away from the image of Andrew's lithe graceful body. For a man who did a lot of his work seated behind a desk, he was in amazing shape. She wanted to ask him how he kept so fit, but decided the question was too personal. She didn't know him well enough to cross the lines dictated by protocal and circumstance.

Randy crouched down in front of the console. "Okay, we're almost there."

Her heart started to beat frantically when she spied the glint of a tail fin through the coral heads. It was almost ghostly in appearance. But when she suddenly saw herself swimming toward the camera, even she had to question what appeared before her. She *did* look like a real mermaid! Randy pressed the pause button, freezing her image in place.

"I can't believe it," she said, shocked.

"My sentiments exactly," Andrew replied in a low voice. "Maybe now you'll understand my enchantment a little better."

Randy looked over his shoulder at her. "Your commercial could sell anything, including squid ink, Lindsay."

"Thanks for the vote of confidence," she said quietly as she got to her feet.

She could feel herself getting too involved with Randy and his father. The last thing she wanted to do was say goodbye, but that was exactly what she was going to do while she still had the strength of will.

"You've just reminded me that I've got an early-morning practice dive. I think I should go before it gets any later."

A strange silence filled the room while Andrew stood to turn on the overhead lights. He leaned against the doorjamb. "Tomorrow's Sunday, your last day of freedom before you start shooting. How would you like to spend part of it snorkeling off Balmoral Island with us? We're packing a lunch."

She lowered her gaze, afraid both he and Randy would detect the explosion of excitement she felt at his invitation. But much as she wanted to accept, she couldn't afford even one more day in this man's company, couldn't handle the emotional consequences.

Andrew moved from the door, his remote expression making it difficult to tell what he was thinking. "You don't have to decide this minute. Just give me a call some time before ten tomorrow."

"N-no, no. I can tell you now." She rubbed damp palms against her hips, an action her host seemed to find of extreme interest. "I'd like to go, but the crew will be arriving en masse tomorrow, and I've got sessions with the costume and makeup artists. I—I don't know when I'll be free, so I can't make definite plans," she stammered.

"You sound like Dad when I call him at the office," Randy muttered, frankly disappointed.

Lindsay held her breath, waiting for Andrew to say something, but he remained silent. Taking the initiative, she said, "This has been a wonderful evening, one I won't forget. Thank you for the dinner, the entertainment and the company."

"It was our pleasure," came the coolly polite response.

Out of nowhere, several security men, including Fernando, appeared at the front door of the villa and preceded her to the limo. With Randy following, Andrew helped her down the steps and into the back seat. "Good night, sweet mermaid," he whispered.

For Randy's sake, as well as her own, she tried to pretend she couldn't feel the slight touch of his father's lips against her hair or the caress of his fingers against her hot skin. Then Andrew let her go and shut the door. Through the glass separating them, she waved to Randy, who smiled and waved back as the limo pulled away from the steps. She forced herself not to take a last lingering look at Andrew.

Already she knew something significant had happened to her, something new and overpowering. When she thought of returning to California, far away from him and his son, a sense of desolation swept over her. It made no sense. Not this soon. And not when she'd been content with her life. Content, that is, until yesterday.

CHAPTER SIX

"ANDREW?" One of the security men poked his head inside the bedroom door. "Phone is for you. It's Clint."

Andrew had heard the phone ring and assumed it was Troy calling Randy. If Clint, his second-in-command, dared disturb him this late, it meant trouble. His eyebrows met in a frown as he picked up the receiver; what he heard didn't sound good. After rapping out instructions and making arrangements, he headed for Randy's bedroom, dreading—dreading for more than one reason—what had to be done.

He found his son in the bathroom brushing his teeth. Randy smiled at him in the mirror above the sink. "She's not only beautiful, she's nice, Dad. Really nice, in all the ways that count. And I have to tell you, you played it just right."

Andrew let out a laugh. "Is that so?" he said, immeasurably relieved by Randy's wholehearted approval. Without it, Andrew would have been deeply disturbed, because he had every intention of seeing more of Lindsay Marshall. And he knew instinctively that she'd wanted to say yes to his invitation for tomorrow.

"Who was on the phone?"

"Clint."

"Uh-oh. Was there an earthquake or a tornado or something?" he asked solemnly, wiping his face with a towel.

"Or something."

Randy dropped the towel on the counter and met his father's eyes. "Don't tell me we've got to go home?"

"I'm afraid so. While we've been gone, a rainstorm has swept a lot of debris into the Truckee River. If it's not cleared out, there's going to be a water shortage in Reno. I've got to get back to survey the damage, see how the cleanup's going—and, if necessary, put our emergency plan into effect."

"Jeez . . ."

Andrew took a fortifying breath. "Do you think I want to leave? Do you have any idea how much I want to see Lindsay again?" The veins stood out in his neck.

Randy finally nodded. "Yeah. I think I do." There was a pause, then he said, "If you want to go over to her hotel right now and say goodbye, Dad, I'll pack up here and meet you at the airport."

Andrew marveled at his son's sensitivity. "Thanks, Randy. But after turning me down, do you think she'll want to see me?"

They stared at each other. "I can guarantee it," Randy said.

On a swell of emotion, Andrew made a playful fist and skimmed Randy's jaw. "What did I ever do to deserve a son like you?"

"I'll think about it and let you know. Good luck, Dad."

Andrew hugged his son, then called his men together to make last-minute arrangements. En route to her hotel, he'd use the limo phone to conduct the rest of his business, so that when he saw Lindsay, he'd be able to concentrate fully on her.

TOO KEYED UP and restless to get ready for bed, Lindsay stood against the patio railing and looked out over the moonlit water. Cutting Andrew out of her thoughts, let alone her life, was proving more difficult than she'd have imagined.

"Lindsay?"

She gasped at the sound of his deep voice and whirled around in astonishment.

It couldn't have been more than an hour since they'd said good-night, yet here he was in her hotel room. She was so happy to see him it frightened her.

He was wearing the same suit he'd worn at dinner, but the tie was missing and his expression had grown sober. Unconsciously, Lindsay held her breath.

"Jake said you were out here. I wouldn't have disturbed you this late if it wasn't important."

A dozen terrifying possibilities flashed through her mind and her pulse raced. "Something's happened. Does this have to do with Randy? Is he all right?"

"No. He's not. And neither am I." His voice trailed off.

She frowned, biting her lip. "Please don't keep me in suspense. Tell me what's wrong."

He moved closer, studying her hair and features as if commiting them to memory. "An emergency has cropped up that demands my immediate return home. Randy's waiting for me at the airport."

Lindsay moaned inside and looked away, afraid he'd be able to see how much his unexpected news had upset her. Even though she'd decided not to spend any more time with him, she couldn't help her reaction, which was swift and intense.

"Poor Randy," she managed to say. "It must be a terrible wrench for both of you, especially since you haven't had a real vacation for so long."

"Interruptions go with the territory. But I have to admit I was surprised at the depth of my disappointment when Clint phoned from Carson City and told me the situation."

She turned to him once more. "Is the emergency life-threatening?"

"The Truckee River is blocked and Reno's facing a water shortage. I'm going to have to inspect it by helicopter, meet with my staff and then decide what steps to take."

The realization that the welfare of Nevada depended on this man and his decisions brought home to Lindsay in a very real way just how important he was. Yet he'd taken precious time from his schedule to see her.

"I—I would have understood if you'd left a message with Jake or Fernando."

"Instead of coming to say goodbye in person?" he said curtly. "No doubt it's what you would have preferred, but unlike you, I deal in honesty."

Heat crept up her neck and face. "What do you mean?"

"Don't pretend you don't know what I'm talking about. You feel the chemistry between us, too. But for some unknown reason, you're afraid of it—afraid of me."

"Th-that's not true," Lindsay stammered. "You saved my life, then you went to great lengths to protect me from any unpleasantness. I'd be less than honest if I didn't tell you how grateful I am for your concern and generosity."

"So it was out of a sense of gratitude that you accepted my dinner invitation this evening—nothing else. Is that what you're saying?"

"Yes." She seized on the opening he'd given her. "That, and a need to make up in some small way for having created adverse publicity for you."

There was a prolonged silence. "Good luck with your commercial, Ms. Marshall. Jake and Fernando have instructions to make sure no one else gets close enough to disturb you during your stay in Nassau. I'll let myself out."

"OKAY, YOU GUYS. This is it. I know we've lost a couple of meets, but Culver City's team isn't that strong. We can beat them any day of the year. Go on out there and show them what you're made of."

While the others got off the bus and hurried into the locker room of the Culver City Swim Club to dress, little Cindy Lou hung back. Lindsay noticed with pleasure that the child's leg was much improved since her swimming therapy had begun. "I'm glad you came home and that no sharks bit you." Cindy Lou curled her hand into Lindsay's.

The mention of the word shark was a painful reminder of the magical evening she'd tried to put out of her mind. "I promised you I'd be here for this meet. Do you think I'd miss seeing you race?" she asked, delighted that Cindy Lou and several other children with special needs had gained enough confidence to perform in front of their peers. "Now run along and get ready so you won't be late."

"Okay."

Lindsay thanked the driver and got off the bus. She found herself wishing once again that she could forget Andrew Cordell and the painful moment on her hotel balcony when he'd walked away.

She'd thought that was what she'd wanted—their interlude brought to an end. No emotional involvement. But it wasn't supposed to hurt this much. Sixteen endless days and nights had passed since that evening. She'd been put through one grueling eighteen-hour workday after another making the commercial, but she hadn't been able to sleep.

Whether she admitted it or not, she'd been waiting for a phone call from Carson City—a phone call that never came. And why would it, when she'd been so dishonest with him? He was much too prominent and busy a man to play foolish games.

Of course, it wasn't a game to Lindsay, but he didn't know that. She wished she could see him again and explain, but the time for explanations had gone. All she had left were her memories and the dozens of newspaper clippings her friends had sent her in jest. Every time she looked at them, she felt a sharp ache as she remembered the man who'd made a brief appearance in her life. And yet, she couldn't stop taking out the clippings and poring over them.

Far too often since her return from the Bahamas she had studied the photograph that accompanied all the articles. It showed the handsome governor of Nevada walking across the hotel foyer carrying her mermaid tail over his arm.

Naturally, her parents had seized on the version appearing in certain less-reputable newspapers that Andrew had stalked her before coming to her rescue. Naturally, this was the version they believed, and they refused to forgive him.

If only they knew how wrong they were about his character, how much he'd come to mean to her in those three short days.

"Hey, Lindsay? Are you coming?" Kyle called to her from the breezeway, interrupting thoughts best left unexamined. "They're ready to start."

Embarrassed to be caught so preoccupied, she hurried over to him, determined to give all her students her complete attention. "Good luck today, Kyle."

He groaned. "We're going to need it."

"I don't think so. I saw you in practice this morning and everybody is swimming well." She walked inside with him and took her place in front of her team, now assembled on the bleachers. The Culver City group sat across the pool from them. After the officials had conferred with her and the opposing team's coach, the meet got under way, starting with the "tadpoles," swimmers aged eight and under.

Little Cindy Lou did her best but couldn't keep up with the competition and came in third to last. As soon as she got out of the pool, she ran limping toward Lindsay with tears glistening in her eyes. When she reached her, she tried to bury her face in Lindsay's lap, but Lindsay wouldn't let her.

"Cindy Lou, last month you came in last. Today you beat two boys on the other team who *don't* have a twisted leg. Do you know how proud I am of you for getting out there and racing with the others?" She hugged her hard. "Everyone's cheering for you. Listen!"

Cindy Lou cocked her head at the sound of both teams chanting, "Way to go, Cindy! Way to go, Cindy!"

A sudden smile transformed her pixie face, and at that moment a male voice said, "Would you ladies look this way, please?"

They both turned their heads at the same time and Lindsay saw a tall, striking blond man in shorts and a T-shirt, not five feet away. He stood there, watching them through the lens of a video camera. When Lindsay realized who it was, she gasped so loud Cindy Lou asked her what was the matter.

"I-it's nothing," Lindsay stammered, feeling lightheaded. By now, many parents on the bleachers had recognized him, and his presence brought a hush to the crowd as he took the few steps necessary to sit down next to her.

His gaze scanned her face relentlessly, almost as if he was hungry for the sight of her. Whether intentional or not, his muscular leg with its dusting of hair brushed against her tanned bare limb, alerting her senses.

"Andrew..." she whispered shakily. The joy of seeing him again robbed her of words and blinded her to everything going on around them. She couldn't think.

Cindy Lou, who'd been so upset minutes before, was now staring at him in undisguised fascination. "Why were you taking pictures of us?"

His smile held a sweetness that took Lindsay's breath away. "Because my son's best friend, Troy, who broke his leg playing high school football, is afraid he can't do any sports now. When I show him what a terrific swimmer you are, he's going to feel foolish."

"My leg came from heaven this way."

"So did your pretty face," he said with such sincerity the little girl smiled. Lindsay could hardly swallow for the lump in her throat. "What's your name?"

"Cindy Lou Markham. What's yours?"

"Andrew Cordell."

"How come you're sitting with my coach?"

Andrew's eyes danced as they met Lindsay's. "Because she's a friend of mine."

"I've never seen you before."

"That's because I don't live here."

"Then how can you be Lindsay's friend?"

"Because we met in the Bahamas."

Her eyes grew huge. "You're the man in the newspaper! You took off her tail so she wouldn't die!"

He flashed Lindsay a silent message. "That's right."

"Did any sharks bite you?"

"No." He grinned. "But a mermaid stole something from me."

His comment made Lindsay's heart skip a beat, and she could almost hear the little girl's mind working everything out. "Cindy Lou, the next heat is ready to start. Hurry up and sit with your group, okay?"

"Okay. See you later. Bye, Andrew." She pecked Lindsay's cheek, then gave him a little wave of her hand before limping off to sit with the rest of the tadpoles.

"I'm sorry I came in late and disturbed you," he murmured. "Ignore me until the meet is over."

That would be impossible, and not only because of the physical contact between them. She could see his security men stationed around the club and knew there were more outside. "How long can you stay?" she whispered.

"I have to be at a charity dinner in two hours."

"In Los Angeles?"

"No. Carson City."

Her eyes closed. How could he do this to her? Didn't he know that if he couldn't stay, it would have been better if he hadn't come at all?

"What are your plans after the meet, Lindsay?"

"Nothing important," she answered too quickly, giving herself away.

"Then drive back to the airport in the limo with me. We have to talk."

She rubbed her hands along her arms in nervous anticipation. "I take it Randy's not with you this time."

While they talked, she pretended interest in the meet and cheered her team on, but in reality, she had no idea who was winning or losing.

"He wanted to come, but he had to work at the scuba shop today. Since our return he's talked nonstop about you and shown the video to all his friends. You already have an active fan club in Nevada."

She bowed her head. "That's nice to hear. When you go back, please tell him how much I enjoyed meeting him." Then in a curious voice, she asked, "How did you know where to find me?"

"I have my sources. Bud Atkins, a private investigator who's a longtime friend, does good research."

His admission put a lot of new thoughts in her head. "Does that mean you know what brand of toothpaste I use?"

"Information of that nature I prefer to gather myself." Lindsay hadn't meant her question to sound provocative and wished she could take it back. He'd caught her completely off guard, confusing her until she hardly knew what she was saying or doing.

"I have to take the bus back to our clubhouse with the kids."

"I'll follow you."

Lindsay sat there dazed, unable to credit that Andrew Cordell had flown all the way from Carson City to talk to her. Over the past two weeks, while she'd been in the Bahamas, he and his staff had been working night and day to solve a water-shortage problem. Yet the most important man in the state of Nevada had left everything behind to come to her swim meet.

And she'd thought she would never see him again.

The swim meet seemed to go on forever, and though she was pleased to see that her team had garnered most of the first-place ribbons, it couldn't be over soon enough for her. Every minute at the meet meant losing precious time with Andrew. Time she needed to explain her behavior that last evening....

Once the children had left the poolside for the lockers she jumped to her feet, aware of Andrew's eyes sweeping her body in intimate appraisal. She wore shorts and a perfectly decent T-shirt, but under his scrutiny, she felt exposed and vulnerable. "I'll see you in Bel Air in about twenty minutes," she said in a breathless voice.

"Hurry." Something in his tone sent her running past people to the locker room, aware that participants and spectators alike were talking about them. All the parents were smiling and before the day was over, everyone from Culver City to Bel Air would know that Governor Cordell had paid Lindsay Marshall a visit. There would be more speculation, more innuendo.

The next half hour turned into a blur. Excited as the kids were over their success, some of the boys in the back of the bus had spotted the two black limousines following them and started to cheer.

Soon every child's gaze was riveted out the windows, and Andrew's visit became the sole topic of conversation. When Cindy Lou blurted out that he was the man from the newspaper picture, the one carrying her mermaid tail, the children besieged her with questions.

When they finally reached the clubhouse, there was the usual mad scramble as the kids got into cars or walked home. When she'd seen the last child out the door, she hurried into the bathroom to look at herself in the mirror.

She wore her hair in a braid and decided it didn't look too bad. She quickly touched up her lipstick and tucked in her T-shirt before she left the clubhouse.

Andrew stood outside next to the limo, talking with one of his men, but when he saw Lindsay he broke off his conversation. He immediately opened the back door to help her inside. "Finally," he murmured, his hand running the length of her arm before he shut the door and went around to the other side.

Between his touch and the emotion in that one word, he had reduced her to a trembling state of longing and tension. What would happen during this totally unexpected, unconventional meeting?

On their way to the airport, he gave the men up front some instructions, then sat back, resting an ankle on the opposite knee. She felt his eyes travel over her. The impulse to lean across the seat and touch him was so overpowering she didn't dare meet his gaze and had to consciously restrain herself by hugging the door.

When she'd left for the meet early that morning, she'd never guessed she'd be driving to the airport with Andrew Cordell. She still had trouble believing he was sitting beside her, making her heart pound so fast and loud she was sure he could hear it.

The tension in the car increased because he still hadn't said anything. *What did he want from her?* When she couldn't stand the suspense any longer, she demanded, "Why didn't you phone?"

"Because I wanted to see your initial reaction for myself."

Lindsay stared at her hands. During those first unguarded seconds by the pool, her joy at seeing him again had been on display for everyone to witness. He could be in no doubt about her feelings now, she mused.

He looked so good, smelled so good. It didn't seem fair that she could feel like this about a man whose life was not only miles but light-years apart from hers.

"I didn't want to leave Nassau," he said, "and I know you didn't want me to go."

She gnawed her bottom lip for a moment as she wondered how to respond. "No. I didn't," she confessed, opting for the simple truth. "But your life is dictated by the demands of your job—and you've chosen that particular job of your own free will. Because you love it. Isn't that right?" She finally turned to look at him and surprised a hardness in his expression that played oddly against his underlying sensuality.

"Is my line of work that abhorrent to you, Lindsay?"

With bowed head she said, "I applaud what you do. It's the lack of privacy, of anonymity, I find appalling. And the controls and restrictions imposed on you and your family—I feel stifled just thinking about them."

He pondered her comment for a few moments. "You've only seen what my life is like in public," he said quietly.

"Is it any different at the governor's mansion?" she asked with more sharpness than she'd intended.

"How would you like to find out?"

Her gaze swerved to his in surprise. "What do you mean?"

"I'm inviting you to come to Carson City as my guest for a few weeks in July."

The invitation to spend time with him in his own home was the last thing Lindsay had expected.

"In case you're worried about propriety, Governor Stevens and his wife and daughters will be there, as well. I've freed up my schedule during that period so

I can relax with Randy and have a vacation at home for a change. We'll go riding on the Circle Q—my brother-in-law's ranch—and camp out at Hidden Lake, my favorite spot. You'd love it."

She had no doubt of it! Suddenly everything was moving much too fast. "That's very generous of you, but I. . . I don't think it would be a good idea."

"You're not indifferent to me," he muttered. "I found that out at the pool. I also know there's no other man in your life. So I have to conclude that my being governor threatens you in some way. But don't forget I'm a man, Lindsay, and that I have a private life, separate from my public one."

"But you're never without your bodyguards."

She heard him sigh deeply. "Such irony. Most women I know seem to consider that a definite plus. But then, I'm forgetting you're a mermaid."

She shifted uncomfortably in the seat. She probably *was* unusual in her dislike of blatant protection, of being followed and watched and guarded. And the mention of other women only disturbed her more.

"I knew about Wendie's illness when I married her, so I made a vow that if I became governor she'd never suffer because of it. To my knowledge, she had all the privacy she craved and never had reason to complain on that score. In fact, she felt comfortable enough to espouse some causes that were important to both of us. Unfortunately the disease defeated her before she could see them through."

"Andrew—" she almost choked getting the words out "—I'm very touched that you'd confide something so painful and personal to me, but you don't begin to understand."

"Then help me."

Taking a deep breath, she said, "You were right in Nassau when you said I feel an attraction. I admit I'm happy to see you. But much as I might like to accept your invitation, there's no point. Not when my career as a marine biologist is going to place me outside your sphere, and not when a serious relationship between us just isn't possible."

She took another deep breath before she could continue. "Coming to your home would only complicate things, and I refuse to hurt Randy. It's better not to start something we can't finish." That was the truth. Not the *whole* truth, but the rest she didn't want to discuss.

An unbearable tension filled the limousine. "I don't believe our careers have anything to do with your fear of getting involved with me. But since you can't or won't tell me what's holding you back, it appears there's nothing more to say. We've arrived at the airport. When I get out of this car, you need never fear I'll disturb you again."

"Now you're angry with me."

"That doesn't begin to cover it," he said bleakly.

Lindsay shivered. It all seemed so hopeless. She was falling—had fallen—in love with him, but she couldn't tolerate his kind of life. And she couldn't give up her hard-won independence or her dreams for the future. The only solution would be to have a brief affair with him, something she couldn't consider, not with him or any other man. For Lindsay, love meant permanence and complete commitment. It meant all or nothing. Besides, Andrew Cordell wasn't the kind of man a woman forgot. Once he got under her skin, he'd stay there. Good heavens, he'd already infiltrated and laid siege. Why lie to herself?

So deep was her turmoil she didn't realize the limo had pulled to a stop in front of the terminal. Andrew was out of the car and ready to walk away before she knew it. He leaned inside, all expression wiped from his face.

"Human nature is a strange thing. I could have sworn something extraordinary happened when I met a certain mermaid. But it seems my mermaid was pure fantasy, after all."

"Wait! Andrew—" she cried, but the door had closed and he had already disappeared into the crowd, surrounded by his security guards.

The driver must have heard her distress because he turned around and opened the glass partition. "Do you want me to call him back, Ms. Marshall?"

Embarrassed that anyone had witnessed her emotional outburst, she said, "No. It wasn't that important, but thank you."

He didn't look as if he believed her, but he nodded, then started the car and pulled away from the curb into the heavy airport traffic, carrying her farther and farther away from the man she'd fallen in love with. The man who could break down her defenses faster than she could build them. Lindsay buried her face in her hands. *What had she done?*

"DAD?" ANDREW'S BODY tautened when he heard his son's voice in the upstairs hallway. He'd hoped to avoid Randy's questions until he'd gotten over the initial shock of Lindsay Marshall's rejection, which was all the more painful because of the things she *didn't* say. The speech he'd given at the Festival of the Arts banquet earlier in the evening was a complete blank in his mind, and he barely even remembered tasting his food.

"Come on in," he called, removing the cummerbund of his tux. Randy breezed into the bedroom, but the expectant smile on his face vanished when Andrew asked him casually how work had gone.

"Something's wrong, isn't it?" Randy insisted.

Andrew lifted his head and their eyes met. "You could say that."

"What happened? Weren't you able to find her or something?"

"Or something," he said, remembering a similar conversation a few weeks ago.

"Wasn't she glad to see you?"

Andrew could still remember the way her eyes had glowed when she'd turned her head and discovered him standing next to her. "She felt the same way I did."

"But?"

"She's afraid."

Randy removed his father's cuff links for him. "I thought she got over that."

"I don't mean she's afraid of me. For some reason, she has an aversion to a high-profile life like mine."

"You're talking about bodyguards and all that stuff."

He shrugged out of his shirt. "That's part of it . . ." *But by no means all.* "None of that matters, Randy, because I won't be seeing her again."

"You mean she wouldn't even consider coming for a vacation? Did you tell her about our plans?"

"I know you can't comprehend anyone giving up a chance to camp out at Hidden Lake," Andrew teased as he hung his tux in the closet, "but it seems our mermaid prefers to swim in her own waters."

Randy followed his father's movements and eyed him compassionately. "I'm sorry, Dad. I was hoping..."

"So was I," Andrew said, surprised by the pain he was feeling. "But the lady isn't interested and has made that clear on several occasions. She was part of our dream vacation. Now it's over.... Listen, I'm bushed. How about you?"

"Yeah. I'm ready to hit the sack."

"Not so fast." Andrew grabbed his son around the neck and gave him a hug. "I always feel better when I've talked to you."

"Same here. If it's any comfort, just remember there are other fish in the sea. So to speak." He gave a halfhearted laugh. "At least that's what you told me when Allison turned me down for the homecoming dance last fall."

"It's small comfort, I realize that now," Andrew said in a low voice, wishing he believed in the age-old adage. He reached up to ruffle his son's hair. "Good night, Randy."

"See you in the morning, Dad."

Knowing it was going to be a long night, Andrew reached for the portfolio containing the figures he was working on. He was trying to reduce the state's growing budget deficit, his number-one priority; tonight, he attacked it with more vehemence than usual. But his concentration lasted all of two minutes and he finally gave up, tossing his papers onto the floor in disgust.

After Wendie's death, he'd immersed himself in work to stave off the pain for short periods of time; he'd discovered that it helped. However the same cure didn't seem to apply in this case—maybe because Lindsay Marshall was very much alive. All he had to do was pick up the phone to hear her voice....

Tempted almost beyond endurance, he got up and headed for the shower.

CHAPTER SEVEN

As soon as Lindsay saw Nate saunter toward her, she got up from the chair where she'd been sitting doing lifeguard duty for the past four hours, relieved to be off duty. The lack of sleep the night before, combined with the oppressive heat, had given her a headache that was getting worse by the minute. If she didn't get home and into bed, she was going to be sick.

"There's someone waiting for you in the office," Nate said, deliberately flexing a muscle, which she ignored, before he sat down in the vacated chair.

Even though she knew it couldn't possibly be Andrew, Lindsay's heart began to pound and she almost ran to the office. Every time she thought of the way she'd let him go yesterday without telling the whole truth, her pain intensified. After what she'd done, he'd never forgive her.

Nate said loud enough for everyone in or out of the pool to hear, "It's not your governor friend!" But her thoughts were on Andrew; nothing else mattered.

When she saw Beth, Lindsay rushed around the end of the counter to hug her friend. "You don't know how happy I am to see you!" She knew she sounded emotional, but she couldn't help it; she was just glad no one else was in the office to eavesdrop on them.

"Word reached Mom that Andrew Cordell showed up at the swim meet yesterday. Then your parents called her, absolutely frantic because they don't trust him and couldn't reach you. They demanded to know what was going on. Mom told them she'd call me to find out what she could, then get back to them."

"I'm sorry you got the brunt of it, Beth, but I couldn't face them until I'd sorted things out in my own mind."

"That's what I figured. Since you didn't return any of my calls, I told my boss I had an emergency and left work early hoping to catch up with you." She scrutinized Lindsay thoroughly. "I never thought I'd say this to you, but you look terrible. What's wrong? I thought you were dying to hear from Andrew Cordell."

"Oh, Beth..." She started to explain, but that was as far as she got before her throat closed up and tears spurted from her eyes. "C-can you come home with me?"

"That's why I'm here. Let's go. I'll follow you back to your apartment."

As sick as she felt, Lindsay realized how much she needed to talk to her friend. Once they had arrived in Santa Monica and were settled in her modest living room, cold drinks in hand, Lindsay told Beth everything that had happened. She began with Andrew's appearance at the swim meet and concluded with the dreadful scene at the airport. "He must despise me by now." Her voice shook and she had to swallow back tears.

"He probably wishes he could," Beth murmured sagely. "It isn't every day a man as important as Andrew Cordell drops everything to show that kind of attention to a woman only to have it thrown back in his face. But then he didn't know what kind of woman he was dealing with, did he?"

Her question made Lindsay uncomfortable, and she squirmed in her seat on the couch. "What do you mean?"

"He hasn't got a clue about the problem with your parents, has he? Or that you've been in therapy? Those are the things you didn't tell him."

After a long interval of quiet Lindsay shook her head. "No. I couldn't tell him. We don't know each other well enough. I—I'm not sure he'd understand." Lindsay jumped to her feet and went into the bathroom to take a couple of aspirin. Beth followed her.

"Well, it's not for want of trying on his part, that's obvious."

Lindsay clutched the sides of the sink and stared at Beth through the mirror, her eyes tormented. "Do you realize he can't even use a rest room without a security guard in attendance?"

"What does that have to do with your feelings for the man? Or has he already proposed to you and you're holding out on me?"

Lindsay averted her face and hurried back into the living room, but she was too agitated to sit down. "He hasn't even kissed me," she admitted in a tremulous voice.

"But you'd like him to. What's the matter? Afraid you'll turn into a pumpkin if he touches you?"

Lindsay smiled through the tears. "I'm afraid I'll never want him to stop. How's that for honesty?"

"It's a beginning." Beth nodded with approval. "Especially when I've never seen you act this way over a man before. Don't forget, you and I go way, way back."

Lindsay's smile faded. "I haven't forgotten anything—particularly not that period when you and your mother had to live with security guards day and night."

"Lindsay—" Beth cocked her head to one side "—you're trying to equate two situations that are entirely different. Mom was being harassed by a lunatic. We were frightened and needed help.

"But Andrew Cordell doesn't live in fear," she went on. "Otherwise he wouldn't have chosen a life in politics. Having bodyguards is a preventive measure. It's meant to be a comfort. Did you resent Jake and Fernando?"

"No. Of course not. But I knew their presence was temporary. If I thought I had to live that way all the time, I couldn't do it. Every move you make has to be planned. You can't do anything spontaneously."

"You mean like diving at sunrise for sharks when the mood strikes you?"

Lindsay stared at her friend. "How did sharks get into this?"

"I don't know. Suppose you tell me? Has it ever occurred to you that choosing a career that puts your safety at some risk is a sign of rebellion against what your parents did to you? Could you unconsciously be punishing Andrew for your parents' mistakes?"

Silence permeated the room. "You sound like a psychiatrist."

Beth got to her feet. "It doesn't require a medical degree to figure out what's going on in your mind, Lindsay. If I were you, I'd take a long hard look at myself. Your parents' fears chased every boyfriend away. But you're an adult now, responsible for your own life. It would be tragic if you allowed yourself to be manipulated by your parents' actions and lost Andrew without even a fight."

Lindsay's eyes closed tightly. "He was never mine to lose."

"No matter what you think, I'd stake my life on the premise that it's not too late to undo the damage. He didn't break away from important state matters and fly to California for a couple of hours merely because he's *fond* of you. For that matter, he didn't get involved in the first place because of just some mild interest. The man has suffered humiliation getting to know you, Lindsay, yet he still showed up yesterday—and suffered even more rejection at your hands."

"Don't say anything else." Lindsay's voice was panicked. "I'm feeling worse with every word you say."

"Good. I'm counting on you to feel so bad you'll do something about it. But I imagine you're going to have to come up with a fairly spectacular plan to win him around. *If* that's what you want," she added quietly.

Lindsay wrung her hands. "I want him, but I want things to stay uncomplicated, and that's not possible. He's not an ordinary man, and in time I'm afraid he'll expect things of me I might not want or be able to give him. We'll end up fighting. Just like I fight with Mom and Dad."

"Ah, now we're getting closer to the truth. So what you're saying is that Andrew Cordell makes unreasonable demands on you, like your parents?" she asked in disbelief.

"Well, yes— No— Not exactly. But—"

"But nothing! Good grief, Lindsay. Give the man a chance!" she shouted as the telephone rang.

Lindsay excused herself and ran to the kitchen to answer it, wishing Andrew was on the other end and knowing he wasn't. Beth trailed behind. When it turned out to be Lindsay's father, Beth whispered, "I'm going to run over to Mom's. Call me there later and we'll talk some more. And for heaven's sake, don't shut Andrew Cordell out of your life. At least give him a chance—unless you're prepared to live with the consequences."

Lindsay gave her friend a hug and, with more calm than she'd felt earlier, dealt with her parents' concerns. She played down Andrew Cordell's visit, all the while thinking about Beth's final admonition. Already the consequences of sending Andrew away a second time had made her physically ill.

After the way she'd treated him yesterday, did she dare approach him to find out if her deepest fears were truly justified?

By the time she'd promised to visit her parents soon and had said goodbye, she was half tempted to call the information operator to get the number of the governor's mansion in Carson City. But fear of rejection made her apprehensive. If she did try to contact him, she'd have to reveal her identity to the person answering the phone. She worried that when Andrew found out who was calling, he'd refuse to talk to her.

Another alternative would be to send a letter, but that seemed too impersonal. She was left with only one solution—go to Carson City and see him in person.

Wasn't that what he'd done by coming to California to visit her? Because he wanted to witness her reaction for himself?

Tomorrow was her day off and the next was the Fourth of July. Two days to drive there and back. Would he even be in town? She knew he spent any free time on his brother-in-law's ranch with Randy. Maybe Beth's mom had connections in Nevada and could make inquiries about where he'd be without giving anything away....

"HEY, DAD! The honor guard and band have already started marching and we're next!"

When Andrew heard that, he broke off his conversation with one of the legislators backing his campaign to reduce waste at the district levels of public education. He glanced at the police escort as he climbed onto the seat of the covered wagon next to Randy and Troy, adjusting his Stetson to keep the sun out of his eyes.

Zack's team of Arabians from the Circle Q Ranch handled well in a crowd, and with a flick of the reins, Andrew urged them forward. They trotted along the main street, to the spectators' approval.

"Everyone in Carson City must've come out this morning for the parade," Troy observed as the boys smiled and waved and whistled at all the pretty girls. Every few yards, Andrew heard his name called out, and he shouted back something appropriate, laughing and exchanging cheerful greetings with people in the crowd.

He supposed this was one of his more pleasurable duties as governor, but a depression had settled over him ever since his return from Los Angeles. His natural zest for living had apparently deserted him, though he tried to camouflage its absence through hard work. The short time he'd spent with Lindsay Marshall had created a yawning emptiness nothing else seemed to fill.

Because Randy knew the underlying reason for his father's mood, he saw through the facade Andrew put on in public. He offered his love and support, which cemented their relationship. Without his son, Andrew couldn't imagine his life making sense.

Now that Troy was part of the family and came for frequent visits, the mansion seemed livelier and Andrew discovered he liked having Alex's brother around. He'd grown very attached to him, especially now that Troy was staying with them while his sister was in the hospital with her new baby, Zackery Sean Quinn IV.

"Hey, you two. Before we go out to the ranch for a picnic this afternoon, let's stop by the hospital and see how little Sean's doing."

"He's great!" Troy grinned. "Zack thinks he looks like Grampa Quinn, and Alex swears he's the image of our dad."

"And what do you think?" Andrew smiled.

"I think he looks funny. His hair sticks out all over and his face is puffy."

"They all look like that when they're first born. You should have seen Randy," Andrew teased, expecting to get a rise out of his son. But for once Randy wasn't paying attention.

"Dad—"

The serious tone in Randy's voice alerted Andrew. "What is it?" he demanded. His keen eyes automatically searched out his security men in the crowd. He poised his body to defend Randy and Troy if it came to that.

"Jeez . . . I think it's Lindsay. Look on the left—by the clown with stilts."

Troy let out a low whistle. "That has to be the mermaid. Nobody else in the world has hair like hers."

Andrew's gaze scanned the crowds and zeroed in on a curtain of molten gold falling from beneath a cowboy hat to the flare of womanly hips. She had come dressed in a denim shirt, jeans and cowboy boots that made the most of her long legs and voluptuous body. His heart slammed into his ribs.

"And you thought it was over," Randy whispered.

"I've got to talk to her before she loses her nerve and runs away." Forgetting where he was or what people would say, let alone the trouble he'd cause his bodyguards, Andrew handed Randy the reins. "Keep on going. Lindsay and I will catch up with you."

"She's not going to run away from you, Dad, not when she's come all this way."

"Well, I'm not taking any chances," Andrew vowed. In one lithe move, he reached the ground and immediately his security guards formed a circle around him.

"Boss? What's going on?" Skip muttered in exasperation.

Andrew kept moving, striding across the blistering hot pavement in his well-worn cowboy boots. "Lindsay Marshall. She's up ahead, about twenty feet."

"Why don't you let us bring her to you? It would be a hell of a lot safer."

But Andrew couldn't think, couldn't breathe. He was only about six feet from her now. She had finally turned her beautiful face in his direction and their eyes met in a long, serious, searching look. Those brilliant, lavender blue eyes took him back to the sunlit waters of the Caribbean.

As he drew closer, he could see the throbbing of a pulse in the hollow of her throat. Her nervousness endeared her to him and brought out his protective instincts.

"Andrew," she whispered, pulling her hands out of her hip pockets in a self-conscious gesture. "I didn't mean to create another scene. I was planning to follow you along the parade route, then speak to you after it was over."

"Then it's lucky Randy spotted you as soon as he did. This way, we don't have to waste another second." He reached for her left hand and grasped it, feeling her rapid heartbeat merge with his.

"Where are you taking me?"

"First, you're going to ride in the covered wagon with my family until the parade's over. And after that, I'm going to find a way to get you to myself where we can be totally alone for a while. Don't tell me how long you can stay. Not yet. I don't want to spoil the enchantment."

He slowed his pace so she could keep up with him, and he noticed how she trembled every time they brushed against each other. As far as he was concerned, it was a credit to his self-control that he didn't simply pick her up in his arms and carry her off to the nearest private spot.

"Lindsay!" Randy shouted and waved his arms when he saw her.

"Hi, Randy!" As she waved back, Andrew closed his hands around her waist, the way he'd been aching to do, and lifted her to the front of the wagon. Troy made room for her by standing behind the seat.

"Why didn't you tell us you were coming? This is great!" Randy positively beamed.

Andrew climbed up behind her and grasped her waist once more, not wanting to give up the curving warmth of her body.

"It was a last-minute decision," came the vague explanation.

"Well, you've made our day," he said with the same kind of emotion Andrew was feeling. "Let me introduce you to Troy. I haven't figured out how we're related, but he's my aunt Alex's brother. She became my aunt when she married my uncle Zack."

"Hello, Troy."

"Hi." Troy's smile was as big as Randy's. "I've been wanting to meet the famous mermaid. How soon till we see you on TV?"

"The ads start in August."

At the pressure of Andrew's hands, she turned her head to look at him. "We're holding up the parade," he said. "Let's sit down so I can drive this thing."

"I'm sorry," she murmured. She watched him trade places with Randy, then sank onto the seat next to him.

His arm went around her back under her hair, and that way he was able to hug her close without anyone's noticing. "I'm not," he whispered beneath the rim of her cowboy hat, inhaling her sweet flowery scent. Suddenly sunshine filled his world again. He couldn't remember the last time he'd been this happy.

They hadn't gone more than a few yards when a reporter from one of the local television stations ran up alongside the covered wagon. "Governor Cordell?" the woman asked. "How about a few words for the folks out here? Everyone wants to know about the lovely lady seated at your side. Isn't she the mermaid you found scuba diving in the Bahamas?"

"Jeez," he heard Randy mutter.

The panic in Lindsay's eyes was all Andrew needed. He gave a private signal to Skip before replying, "She's a friend of the family, here to enjoy Carson City's Fourth of July festivities along with the rest of us. My congratulations to the excellent parade committee, who always make this day so memorable."

He waved his hat amidst a barrage of flashes, then sat back, pulling Lindsay close once more, gratified by the way she nestled into his arms. He knew perfectly well that her being at the parade was no coincidence, and he couldn't get her alone fast enough to suit him.

The newspaper reporter wanted more, but thanks to Andrew's security men who surrounded her, she didn't get a chance to ask further questions.

Lindsay had to remind herself that she'd come to Carson City of her own free will and should have been prepared for anything. But she hadn't counted on the thunderclap of excitement she'd felt at seeing Andrew again or the uncontrollable urge to touch him, whether they had an audience or not.

She wasn't surprised that the media would pounce on her unexplained appearance with the governor. What frightened her was the intensity of her own feelings. It was all she could do not to wrap her arms around Andrew and cling to him in plain sight of everyone.

Dressed in a dark blue Western-cut jacket and jeans, a faded Stetson atop his head, he looked so much a part of his Nevada heritage, so natural and handsome, she found it almost impossible to stop staring at him each time she turned her head in his direction to wave to the crowd.

"How long can you stay, Lindsay?" Randy wanted to know. She felt Andrew's eyes on her, waiting for her answer.

"I drove here, so I'll have to start back by six tonight. Swim-team practice starts at eight-thirty sharp tomorrow morning."

"Then you'll have time to fly to the ranch with us after the parade. We're going riding, and there'll be a barbecue out on the range with Uncle Zack and his friend Miguel."

Troy said, "Maybe you'll have time to swim with us and show me some exercises I can do with my leg? No one's going to certify me for scuba diving until it gets a lot stronger. Andrew showed me some pictures of that little girl you've been coaching, and I thought that—"

"I'd be thrilled to help you."

"Boys, hold on there. Give Lindsay a chance to breathe."

"Maybe you ought to take your own advice," Randy teased, bringing a blush to Lindsay's face. But Andrew didn't let her go. The spot where his hand caressed the curve of her hip with disturbing urgency was on fire. Nobody but the boys could see what he was doing, and he was taking full advantage of it. She didn't mind. All she could think about was being alone with him.

To distract herself, she turned her head to talk to Randy. "You'd better know I've never ridden a horse before."

"You're kidding!" both boys replied in unison.

She caught Andrew's smile out of the corner of her eye. "I'm afraid I'm more at home with fish than animals," she teased, "so don't laugh at me if I fall off the saddle the first time around."

It was on the tip of her tongue to tell them about the spinal injury that had prevented her from participating in any sports all through her teen years and early twenties. But she decided this wasn't the time or the place.

"You won't. Trust me," Troy assured her. "Besides, anyone who swims with sharks has to be well coordinated."

At the mention of the word "shark," Lindsay felt Andrew's hand stiffen against her body, and she immediately regretted having begun this conversation. She'd forgotten how sensitive he was on the subject. Obviously he didn't want his son getting any more ideas about going into marine biology.

She quickly changed the subject, pointing to a huge black rubber crow sailing through the air from a tether. "What's that?"

"The mascot of one of our local radio stations," Andrew murmured. But Lindsay wasn't listening, because his mouth was only a few inches from hers and she didn't know if she'd be able to restrain herself much longer. She needed Andrew's kiss more than she needed air to breathe.

Throughout the rest of the parade, the boys did most of the talking—a good thing, in Lindsay's opinion, since she doubted she was still capable of coherent speech. Andrew's nearness, the warmth of his hard body, his exciting masculine scent—it all enfolded her like an invisible cloak.

Perhaps because of the chemistry between them or perhaps because he sensed the depth of her entrancement, he didn't try to involve her in further conversation. Instead, he kept her molded to his side and bantered with the boys while he waved to the crowds.

By the time they reached the city park where the parade ended, her desire for him had turned into physical pain. Even her palms ached. She didn't dare look at him as he reached for her and swung her easily to the ground. The next thing she knew, his hand had stolen beneath her hair to the back of her neck. Gently stroking her tender skin, he guided her to the limousine parked a few feet away.

But once the four of them were seated inside, Andrew removed his hand and no longer attempted to sit close to her. She thought she knew why. If his emotions were as raw as hers, it was necessary to put a little distance between them in front of the boys, at least during the trip to the ranch.

"Where's your car parked?" he asked.

"By the mall."

"Do you need anything from it?"

"No."

He turned to Randy and Troy. "Is there some reason either of you needs to go back to the mansion?"

They shook their heads and Randy said, "If Lindsay's going to see the ranch, we shouldn't waste any more time around here."

"We can run to the hospital tonight after she leaves," Troy added.

"Hospital?" She turned to Andrew for an explanation, but he was giving instructions to his driver.

"My sister had a baby boy yesterday morning," Troy supplied.

"That must be exciting for you."

"Yeah. It's kind of fun to think I'm an uncle."

That comment brought up the question of how Randy was related to the new baby, and for the rest of the drive to the small airport, the boys kept Lindsay entertained with a lighthearted discussion of complicated family relationships. It helped curb the unbearable need to throw herself into Andrew's arms.

When she had seen the crowd part for him and had watched him walk toward her, she'd almost melted from the fire in his eyes. Until that moment, part of her had been frightened that he wouldn't want anything to do with her; one look at his expression and she knew nothing had changed for him.

Though she marveled at the sight of so many cattle and the deep green alfalfa fields below them, her attention was on the man strapped in the copilot's seat in front of her. Right now she was so happy to be with him, the flight to the Quinn ranch in the yellow eight-seater plane barely registered.

CHAPTER EIGHT

"IT LOOKS LIKE Pete and the guys have already left for the north fork to join in the barbecue!" Troy exclaimed as the four of them got out of a Circle Q van and entered the stable, which was ten minutes from the landing strip. "I'll get Cotton Candy for you, Lindsay. Zack says she's the gentlest, most surefooted little mare on the ranch, and she'll be perfect for your first ride."

"Thanks, Troy."

Lindsay deduced from the boys' conversation that the stable was the first place Zackery Quinn had put Troy to work after hiring him the summer before. He'd learned his job well and evidently worshiped his new brother-in-law.

"Since it's going to take a little time for Lindsay to get used to being on a horse, why don't you guys saddle up and head out," Andrew suggested. "I'll introduce her to Cotton Candy and we'll catch up with you."

She could sense the unspoken communication running between Randy and his father. "Right, Dad. We'll see you later. Let's go, Troy."

After they'd moved farther into the barn to get their horses, Andrew turned to Lindsay, his features partially hidden by the rim of his hat. "Wait here a moment while I get a saddle from the tack room."

"All right," she murmured, growing more and more impatient to be alone with him. She inhaled the warm pungent smell of horses and hay. From the moment she'd entered the plane until she'd driven to the stable, everything she'd observed about the Circle Q told her that the owner loved this land. He clearly took great pride in every aspect of his enormous working ranch.

She understood from the boys that because Randy's mother had been half owner of the Circle Q, the inheritance had fallen to Randy who, as of a few weeks ago, was a full partner with his uncle.

Lindsay hadn't been able to resist doing a little research on Andrew back home in California. She'd gleaned information about him from several newspapers and magazines, learning that the Cordell family had originally made its money in sheep ranching. Investments over the years had made him independently wealthy, and he didn't have to rely on donations from various interest groups to fund his election campaigns.

Her admiration for Andrew grew when she realized that he could have squandered his fortune the way so many movie stars had done. Instead, he'd been a brilliant scholar who had finished high school early and gone to Yale on a full academic scholarship. Early in his undergraduate days, he'd married Wendie Quinn and they'd had a baby, none of which had prevented him from attending law school. After graduation he'd practiced law in a private firm and eventually become a district attorney.

Now he was serving a second term as governor, and Lindsay wouldn't be surprised if destiny took him to Washington. From every indication, Andrew was a hardworking, dedicated public servant, honestly concerned about the direction his state was headed. He would leave an enviable legacy behind, one that transcended money and power.

He was also a loving father whom Randy adored. She'd observed how close they were when she met them in the Bahamas. Randy was growing up to be a responsible and appealing young man; he and Troy and baby Sean would all share in the heritage that turned out great men and leaders like the Quinns and the Cordells.

More than ever, she marveled at her chance meeting with Andrew at the dive site and again wondered at her temerity in showing up at the parade unannounced.

Thanks to Beth, who'd made a phone call to the governor's mansion, Lindsay had discovered that Andrew would be part of the Fourth of July festivities. Once she knew where to find him, she'd needed no further incentive to drive to Nevada. But now that she was here, she was nervous.

The sound of horse's hooves thudding on the packed-dirt drive drew her attention, and she wandered over to the door to watch the boys ride out. Except for hearing that Zack Quinn bred Arabians, she knew nothing about horses. Yet her eye could appreciate the spirit and beauty of their sorrel-colored mounts as they galloped away, young cowboys at home in the saddle.

Without warning, a hand shot past her shoulder and pushed the door closed. Lindsay whirled around in surprise and came face-to-face with Andrew, who was now hatless. He braced his other hand against the door, trapping her in place.

The heat generated by their bodies proved too heady for Lindsay, who could hardly catch her breath. She backed against the door to stay upright. But she needn't have worried; Andrew followed with his powerful body until they were virtually molded to each other.

"Andrew!" she cried in a strangled whisper.

"Do you have any idea of the kind of control it took to keep from grabbing you in front of the boys?"

His words filled her with elation. He'd purposely avoided contact with her because he couldn't trust himself in front of Troy and Randy!

"A man can only take so much. I hope this is why you came to Carson City, because if it isn't, it's too late now."

He lowered his head and covered her mouth with his, parting her lips with breathtaking urgency. His hungry kiss deepened in an explosion of feeling. It aroused a burning desire inside Lindsay that released any lingering inhibitions. She felt like a drowning victim who had suddenly surfaced and could take in life-giving air. Lindsay went where Andrew led, needing his strength.

Floating in sensual ecstasy, she wound her arms around his waist, craving an even closer intimacy. She'd been wanting this for so long, in truth, ever since they'd been closeted together in that small room behind the hotel's reception desk in Nassau.

She lost all awareness of time passing and was driven by the mindless passion his hands and lips created, uncaring that her hat had tumbled to the floor.

"You're so beautiful, Lindsay. I can't believe I have you in my arms at last."

Somehow, their positions had changed. This time, his back was to the door, his strong legs cradling hers. They exchanged one prolonged kiss after another, and for Lindsay, each kiss felt natural, inevitable. She forgot that she'd ever felt apprehensive about him.

Her softer body melted against his body. She couldn't get enough of him and clung to his mouth, driven by age-old instinct, by needs she'd never experienced in another man's arms.

"I want you," he murmured in a husky voice.

"I want you, too," she confessed in a fever of excitement, too far gone to realize what she'd said.

She heard his tortured groan, then tore his lips from hers and put her at arm's length, caressing her upper arms with restless energy. Naked longing blazed in his eyes. "If I kiss you one more time, so help me I won't be able to stop and we'll end up in the hay, which is the last place I have in mind for us."

Lindsay shook her head to clear it. The desire he'd aroused prevented her from saying anything. It was all she could do to regain control of herself.

He shook her gently, causing the gold silk of her hair to undulate against her body. "You make me feel like a lovesick boy in the first throes of passion." He threw back his head in a gesture that might have signaled ecstasy or despair. "I'm thirty-seven years old, and I left the schoolroom a lifetime ago. I have a grown son I love and responsibilities I can't shirk. But right now—" his fingers bit into her shoulders "—I can't think beyond losing myself in you." He sounded like a man who couldn't take any more. "Do you understand what I'm saying, what I'm feeling?"

"Yes!" She finally managed to give him her heartfelt answer, and it produced another shuddering groan from him.

"You realize it's going to be impossible for me to behave myself around you from now on, don't you? We're long past due at the barbecue and I couldn't care less—because I don't want to share you with anyone else."

Lindsay moaned because she knew exactly what he meant. Since her trip to the Bahamas, Andrew had been the focus of her world and nothing else seemed to matter.

"Maybe I shouldn't have come. All I ever do is disrupt your life." In an attempt to think rationally, Lindsay pulled out of his arms, turned and started to reach down for her cowboy hat. But Andrew prevented her from completing the motion and dragged her back against his chest, running his hands over her hips and stomach with increasing urgency.

"You've disrupted my life all right, since the moment you swam through that gulley into the light." He sounded out of breath. "How in the world am I going to make it through the next few hours, talking intelligibly with my family and friends, when my body is screaming to make love to you?" he murmured. "I'm not talking about this frenzied kind of kissing and touching. I mean really loving you in the privacy of my bedroom, without worrying about time or deadlines or responsibilities."

"I-I've been asking myself the same thing. But I could never have an affair with you, Andrew, no matter how much I want to be with you."

He whirled her around, his mouth hard. "If that had been my intention, I would have taken you to a motel when I came to visit you in Culver City. I know I could have persuaded you."

She lifted haunted eyes to his. "You probably could have." Swallowing nervously, she said, "I don't seem to have any control over my emotions when I'm around you, either. During the parade—" She broke off, deciding it was better to say nothing.

"There's only one solution that makes any sense," he whispered against her lips. "And that's never to see each other again."

Her horrified reaction must have told him what he wanted to know. He let out an exultant cry and crushed her in his arms, burying his face in her fragrant hair.

"Don't you realize I only said that because I had to know how you really felt before I asked you to marry me?" Lindsay gasped and lifted her head to look at him, wondering if she'd only imagined what he'd just said.

"Why do you look so surprised? Did you think I flew to California because I didn't have anything better to do?"

In a state of shock she whispered, "We hardly know each other."

His hands rested on her shoulders and he leaned down to kiss her eyelids and nose. "You're wrong. We know the most important thing. We love each other. You love me, or you wouldn't have come to see me today. And I love you, my elusive mermaid. You've enchanted me and I want to make you my wife as soon as possible. We'll have years and years to learn everything there is to know about each other. In the meantime, I want to go to bed with you every night. I want to have more children. I want to live, Lindsay. Really live. But only with you."

"Andrew..." She cried his name softly, too overcome by emotion to continue.

"It's bad enough to worry that some unknown merman could attract your attention and carry you off to his undersea grotto," he whispered. "And I'm terrified a sea witch might come looking for you. But even worse is my fear that a shark could decide to make a meal of you and you'd be lost to me forever." He tightened his hold. "I refuse to let that happen."

It was starting to sink in that out of all the desirable, suitable women in the world who would give up anything and everything for the joy of being loved by him, he had proposed marriage to *her*. "But you're the governor and you require a wom—"

"Shh." He silenced her words with his mouth until they were both trembling. Then he slid his arms around her and rocked her back and forth. "Let's ride to the north fork and make an appearance at the barbecue. After a decent interval, we'll leave for Carson City. I want you to spend the night at the mansion with Randy and me. It will give you an opportunity to see how we live."

"But—"

"First thing in the morning I'll put you on a plane. One of my men will drive your car back to California and leave it at the L.A. airport in time for you to get to the swim club by eight-thirty."

The rocking stopped.

"Don't say no, Lindsay. You owe it to both of us to learn as much as you can about me while you're here."

He was right. This was why she'd come....

Slowly she nodded. While she stood wrapped in his arms, she wanted nothing more than to stay this close to him forever and forget the world.

"Thank God," His voice shook and his mouth descended once more in a deep slow seductive kiss that left her weak. Her arms slid convulsively around his waist, her body registering the sensual feel of hard-muscled flesh that was hot to the touch.

When he slowly put her from him, she didn't understand what was happening. She swayed on her feet, grasping his wrists for support. "One more second of this," he murmured huskily, "and I won't be able to take another step, let alone get on my horse."

She knew what he meant. Her limbs felt liquified and heavy; her breathing was erratic. "I...I didn't know it could be like this," she admitted in a daze.

When his fingers reached out and traced the swollen contours of her mouth, her body responded with an involuntary quiver of yearning.

His eyes darkened in intensity. "What we share is something so precious and rare few people ever experience it, Lindsay."

She knew he spoke the truth. And though it took every shred of willpower, she let go of his arms and stepped away on unsteady legs.

She'd had several boyfriends over the years and in college had fallen hard for Greg, but they'd never reached this stage. She'd never wanted to go to bed with him, never wanted to blot out the world and satisfy this hunger, this craving. In retrospect, she realized that his kisses hadn't created the burning need to merge with him, to lose herself in him, uncaring where they were or what was going on around them. If a caress from Greg *had* made her body pulse in yielding delight, she knew now she would have defied her parents and spent that vacation in La Jolla with him.

Feigning a brightness she didn't feel, she picked up her hat and put it on her head, fastening the ties beneath her chin. Afraid to look at him for fear she'd fling herself into his embrace, she said, "I'm ready to ride. All I ask is that you don't laugh at me. It's easy to be graceful in the water, but riding a horse is going to be another matter."

"You no longer have a mermaid's tail, so I don't anticipate any problem," came the low reply. "Let's get out of here before I drag you over to that corner and ravish you."

His hand slid beneath her hair to rest on the back of her neck, and they walked out to the paddock where the horses were tethered and waiting. Lindsay was on the verge of begging him to carry her back inside when she caught sight of two mounted men some distance away. *Andrew's bodyguards.*

Suddenly the delight went out of the day. For a little while, she'd forgotten about them. She'd forgotten everything because she'd been beguiled by the overpowering attraction between her and Andrew.

But he'd known his men were just outside, that they could walk in at any moment, invading their privacy. Andrew's life wasn't his own. That was why he'd been able to pull away from her before they'd gone any further.

"Forget they're there." He read her mind with astonishing ease as he helped her up into the saddle of the gray-and-white mare. "Unless our lives were threatened, they would never come into the barn without permission."

On that succinct remark, he placed the reins in her hands and adjusted her stirrups, then mounted his own stallion who pranced in place. After shoving his hat on his head, he turned to her.

"Before that overactive imagination of yours misconstrues anything else, let's get something straight. You're too important to me—I'm not just going to make love to you in the first convenient spot that crops up. I have a few scruples left. I want to make you my wife before I touch you the way I'm aching to do. But make no mistake—" his voice took on a determined note "—when you do become my wife, we'll make love whenever and wherever we feel like it, and I promise you, we won't be worrying about the rest of the world." His words brought a blast of heat to her face that had nothing to do with the scorching sun overhead.

"A gentle pat on the hindquarters is all your horse needs. Hold the reins with a firm grip so she knows you're in charge, but give her enough slack to move her head."

Thankful to be forced to concentrate on something besides Andrew's marriage proposal, Lindsay did as he suggested. She let out a surprised cry of delight when the docile horse began to walk.

"You're doing fine. Now take her around the paddock to get used to her. Just pull the rein when you want to change direction, and she'll follow your lead."

By the time she'd made a complete circle, Lindsay had lost some of her nervousness. Andrew flashed her a brilliant smile that melted her bones and lent her confidence. Finally she announced she was ready, and side by side they headed out.

As they followed the dirt track that ran between deep green fields of sweet-smelling alfalfa, Andrew told her about the Walker River, which ran through the property.

Fascinated by his accounts of the native peoples who once flourished in the area, Lindsay ignored the low back pain that had started the moment she'd mounted Cotton Candy. She assumed her discomfort was natural because she'd never been on a horse before, so she didn't mention it to Andrew.

Though the heat from a cloudless blue sky burned its way through her shirt to the skin of her shoulders, she thought it was the most beautiful day of her life. For a little while she managed to pretend that there weren't any security men in front of them and behind them.

Eagerly she plied Andrew with dozens of questions, greedy to know every detail of his life. She felt a desperate need to catch up on all the years she'd missed, all the experiences that had turned him into the man he was today.

She thought he might not want to dicuss Wendie. But as soon as Lindsay broached the subject, he satisfied her curiosity without acting the least bit uncomfortable. Knowing he'd had a happy marriage reassured Lindsay. It meant that he was capable of deep enduring love; it meant he was motivated to work hard at marriage, to experience that kind of emotional fulfillment again. She knew too many people on the Hollywood scene—like Beth's mother—whose marriages had failed, and unfortunately most of them carried around a lot of pain and guilt because of it.

Andrew didn't seem plagued by past regrets, except for his emotional neglect of Randy after Wendie's death, and he was more than making up for that now.

Soon they'd left the cultivated fields behind, and a vast sweep of rangeland spread out before them. In the distance she could see the piñon pines dotting the majestic Sierra Nevadas and the tall Russian olive trees lining the riverbank. Andrew followed her gaze.

"We're almost there. I think my mermaid has developed her land legs now and is ready for a gallop. Want to try?" He looked as excited as a schoolboy, and though the pain in her back was much worse than before, she didn't have the heart to disappoint him.

"What do I do?"

"Pat her again and follow my lead. Always keep a firm grip on the reins but give her her head. If you want to stop, simply pull back on the reins and she'll come to a standstill."

Lindsay nodded, hoping Andrew wouldn't notice her difficulty in sitting straight in the saddle.

"Let's go!" He made a clicking sound between his teeth, and his horse broke into a gallop. With fluid grace he and the stallion flew over the ground, looking as if they'd just materialized out of an old Western movie.

Anxious to please Andrew, who was doing everything in his power to make this a memorable outing, she determined to see this through, no matter how much pain she was in. Gritting her teeth, she put her hand back and patted the horse's rump. That was when she felt a sharp stabbing pain shoot through her hips and down her legs.

Her cry startled the horse, who took off like an arrow in flight. Every time her hooves touched the ground Lindsay's pain intensified.

By now Andrew had reined in his stallion and had turned in the saddle to watch Lindsay's progress. When he saw that her horse was out of control, he called to her in an urgent voice, telling her to pull back on the reins.

The pain had made her so nauseated she was afraid she was going to be sick. The reins slid out of her hands and flapped against the horse's neck while she held on to the pommel. Every movement of Cotton Candy's sent excruciating pain through her body. She tried to stand in the stirrups but had no feeling in her legs.

With a sense of déjà vu, she remembered the horror of waking up from the bus crash with no feeling below her waist. *"Oh, no,"* she whispered in anguish. *"No!"* She was only vaguely aware that Andrew had ridden up to her and caught the reins to bring Cotton Candy to a stop.

"Lindsay! What is it?"

Like lightning he leapt from the saddle, his face white with fear.

"Andrew!" she screamed in terror before he caught her rigid body in his arms. "Andrew..." She cried his name one more time before fainting dead away.

CHAPTER NINE

"DAD?"

When he heard Randy's troubled voice, Andrew looked up through bleary eyes to see his son enter the cubicle off the emergency room. Skip stood outside the curtains to guard against any curiosity seekers. "Uncle Zack flew me and Troy in. They're waiting outside. What happened? What's wrong with Lindsay?"

Andrew rose to his feet and gave Randy a hug. "I'm glad you're here. It's going to be a while before we know anything. She's in X ray right now."

While Andrew straddled the only chair, Randy perched on the examining table. "All Uncle Zack said was that she'd fainted and you were flying her to the hospital in the helicopter."

He rubbed the back of his neck in a weary gesture. "I'm afraid there's a lot more to it than that. She injured herself riding and her legs have gone numb."

Randy's frown deepened. "Is it serious, Dad?"

"Lord, I hope not." He got up from the chair, unable to stay seated. The way she had cried his name before passing out would haunt him all his life. "I should never have taken her riding. When she told us this would be her first time on horseback, I should have realized there was a reason."

"Why? I know lots of people older than Lindsay who've never been on a horse."

As always, Randy took a common-sense approach, and as always, Andrew appreciated it. He gave his son a grateful smile before he continued. "After I checked her in, I got hold of Bud, who tracked down her parents' unlisted phone number in Bel Air. I called to inform them their daughter was in the hospital. They fell apart, Randy. Accused me of everything in the book."

"You're kidding!"

"I wish I was. It seems that when Lindsay was eleven, she was in a near-fatal bus crash that resulted in a spinal injury and paralysis of her lower limbs."

"Lindsay?" Randy was astonished.

Andrew nodded. "I know. After watching her mermaid routine, it's hard to imagine her in that condition. She underwent surgery several times to repair the damage to her spine, and it took years before she learned to walk again. She had to be tutored at home most of her teenage life. Swimming proved to be the best therapy, which is why she's such a strong swimmer today."

"Jeez, do you think—"

"Don't say it," Andrew broke in.

Randy jumped off the table and gripped his father's shoulder. "It's not your fault, Dad, no matter what her parents say."

Andrew's face contorted in lines that made him appear older than his thirty-seven years. "The hell it isn't. I should have left her alone from the very beginning. Because of my selfish desire to know her, she almost drowned. Because of my negligence, she could be paralyzed again, possibly for the rest of her life!"

Randy stared hard at his father. "No one forced Lindsay to have dinner with us at the villa, and no one forced her to come to the parade today. Accidents happen. No one's to blame."

A long silence ensued. "You're right," Andrew conceded, running his hands through his hair. "But it's impossible to remain objective at a time like this. I'm in love with her, Randy. After your mom, I didn't think it could happen again, and certainly not this fast, but it did."

"I know, because I watched it happen, and I'm glad. If you want my opinion, she's in love with you, too. Troy agrees. He says you two act exactly like Uncle Zack and Aunt Alex. They never notice other people when they're together, either."

After eyeing his son for a moment, Andrew said, "I want you to be the first to know that I asked Lindsay to marry me today."

A sunny smile broke out on Randy's face, erasing any fears Andrew might have harbored over his son's ability to accept another woman into their lives. "What took you so long?"

Randy's question broke some of the tension, and with a gruff laugh, Andrew tousled his hair. "You need to know the rest. She hasn't given me an answer, and something tells me she's going to refuse, particularly now that this accident has happened."

"That doesn't make sense! Not when she loves you."

"I don't understand it, either...." Andrew's voice trailed off. "But I intend to uncover the truth, no matter how long it takes."

"Boss?"

Andrew's gaze darted to Skip, who'd poked his head inside the cubicle. "Is she back?"

"Yes. The doctor says you can visit her now."

"Good luck, Dad. We'll all be waiting."

Andrew followed his son into the corridor and hurried toward the examining room where they'd first brought Lindsay. The last time he'd seen her, she'd been unconscious, her beautiful face pinched white from the pain she'd suffered.

His heart leapt in his chest when he slipped behind the curtain and saw that she was wide awake, lying flat against the mattress. Her color had improved and her golden hair splayed over the hospital bed. It made her look like a princess in a fairy tale. Like a mermaid stranded on the beach.

"Andrew..."

He reached her side in an instant, hoping she'd extend her hand, anything to show she was glad to see him. If eyes were the mirror of the soul, then hers reflected anguish, and it tore him apart. He wanted to climb onto the bed with her and hold her in his arms, comfort her. "Are you still in pain?"

"No. They've given me something for it." Suddenly tears filled her eyes. "Forgive me for making such a spectacle of myself. All I do is hurt and embarrass you. Now I've taken you away from your family and ruined your holiday."

He leaned down and smoothed the hair away from her temples, kissing her quiet. He prayed it was the medication that prevented her from responding. "There's nothing to forgive. I love you, Lindsay. All I want is for you to get better."

She turned her face toward the side curtain, away from him. "You've been wonderful to me. I didn't mean to spoil our outing." Her voice quavered as she spoke. "Poor Cotton Candy. My screams must have terrified her."

Taking a fortifying breath, he said, "Why didn't you tell me about your back injury?"

Her head whipped around. "How did you know about that?" she asked defensively. "Oh, yes. Your private investigator. He must be good."

She was upset, exactly as she'd been that night in Nassau, when she'd called in the police to question him. He couldn't understand what prompted such abrupt changes in her.

"Your parents told me."

Her face blanched, and he knew immediately something was wrong.

"You've talked to my parents?"

"Naturally. I phoned them as soon as you were taken into the emergency room."

"Why?" Again, the voice of anguish, and if he wasn't mistaken, panic.

"Because they're your family. They're entitled to know their daughter's in the hospital. I promised I'd call them back as soon as we know the extent of your injuries."

She gave a tortured moan. "You shouldn't have done that. You had no right! I'm twenty-seven years old and I don't need you or anyone else worrying about me, taking over my life and making decisions for me. I'm not a little girl anymore!"

He felt as if he'd just been kicked in the stomach. But he wasn't about to let this go, because he had an idea he was getting closer to the truth about her unexplained fears. "Is that what you think I've been doing? Trying to control you?"

"You did it when you assigned me bodyguards, when you changed my room. You do it with Rand—" She broke off.

Baffled and intrigued, he said, "Yes? What about my son?"

"I—I shouldn't have said anything. It's none of my business." She closed her eyes and turned her face away once more.

"I'm making it your business. Tell me what I do to Randy. Please, Lindsay. This is important to me. Help me understand what's going on inside you."

Tears escaped her eyelids and trickled onto the sheet. "When Randy found out I was going to study sharks, he got excited and said it was what he'd like to do. You immediately changed the subject."

With his mind racing ahead, Andrew tried to figure out exactly what she was saying. "That's true. Sharks are dangerous, and the thought of what they can do to a human being isn't particularly pleasant."

She faced him again. "But if Randy's gone so far as to become a scuba diver, if he intends to pursue a career in marine biology, then no matter how you feel about it, it's *his* life, *his* decision."

Andrew blinked. "That's true, and if he wanted to become a shark expert, I wouldn't stand in his way. But right now Randy doesn't have a clue what he wants to do for a living. Before he took up scuba diving, he was in the mail-order business and imagined himself a *Forbes* tycoon. Since our return from the Bahamas, he and Troy have been talking about becoming ranchers together. Two months into college, and he'll probably decide to take up the bassoon and play in the symphony."

He thought that'd get a little smile out of her, but all she did was stir restlessly.

"My parents used to pretend I didn't know what I was talking about, didn't know what I wanted, because they couldn't handle the truth. They bristled just the way you do every time the subject is brought up. Randy can't help but notice the change in your behavior."

"Lindsay—" He half laughed, half cried in exasperation "—it wasn't Randy I was worried about. It was *you.* When Pokey told me you were swimming The Buoy, I shuddered. No man in love with a woman wants to think of her in danger. As for switching rooms and assigning men to guard you, I did that to ensure your safety, your privacy. Knowing the press had gotten hold of the incident, I didn't dare leave you to the mercy of boorish curiosity seekers who enjoy harassing celebrities."

She took a long time before answering. Finally she said, "You sound like my parents. They've always done what they thought was best for me, too. They're overprotective because they're afraid something will happen to me. It's an irrational fear that started years ago, after my accident. Except for Beth, who stood up to them, they ruined every relationship I ever had to make sure I stayed home, safe and protected."

Frustration welled up in Andrew. "Don't compare me to your parents, Lindsay. From the sound of it, they need professional help. But right now is not the time to go into it. Why don't you try to sleep? Let the sedative do its work."

"I don't want to sleep," she murmured. "Regardless of your motives, the end result is the same. In Nassau you decided to shield me from danger by making decisions *you* considered in my best interests. You didn't discuss them with me, and when I objected, you over—"

"Because the situation demanded it," he interrupted forcefully, trying to reason with her. "Are you telling me you wouldn't be concerned for my safety if you knew a real threat existed?"

"I'd be terrified," she confessed, giving him that much at least. "The possibility of... of assassination is always present, and it terrifies me. But I wouldn't ask you to step down as governor because of it. I wouldn't try to control where you go, what you do. I wouldn't do your thinking or make your decisions for you."

The adrenaline rushed through his veins. "Is that what I've been doing?"

"You called my parents without asking me if I wanted you to."

His hands curled into fists. "Because I didn't know the extent of your injuries and I assumed you'd want their support in case you needed surgery."

Her eyelids were too heavy; she could no longer look at him. "You should have discussed it with me first. They're the *last* people I would have wanted to know about this. Not because I don't love them, but their phobia—"

"Lindsay." He took a steadying breath. "You were brought here in excruciating pain and taken immediately to X ray. The doctor who first examined you didn't rule out the possibility of surgery. Because you're in my care, I felt an obligation to inform your parents. If you were a parent, you'd understand. Even when I'm an old man, I'll want to be notified if something serious happens to Randy."

"I'm not in your care!" she almost screamed. "I came to Carson City because the last time we parted, I was rude, even though I hadn't meant to be, and I wanted to explain. Don't you see?" She shook her head and covered her eyes with the back of her arm. "You take charge without giving it a thought. It's as normal to you as breathing. A marriage between us would never work."

Andrew felt the blood drain from his face. "You don't know what you're saying!"

"My parents always say that when they're angry." Her voice was hoarse. "Andrew, if we get married and I go on pursuing my career in marine biology, can you honestly say it won't become an issue between us? That you won't demand I give it up without question or argument and be a conventional wife? You've already told me you hate the mere idea."

"I do," he admitted through clenched teeth, but at that moment the attending physician pushed the curtains aside and entered the cubicle. He nodded to Andrew, who refrained from saying anything else to Lindsay. He didn't want to upset her any further, not right now.

"What do the X rays say?" Andrew got directly to the point, still reeling from his exchange with Lindsay. It had affected him like a kick from a wild horse.

"That's the good news, Governor." Then he walked over to the bed and smiled down at his patient. "There's no damage. It's my opinion that, because you'd never been horseback riding before, you put too much strain on muscles you'd never used quite that way, and they went into spasm as soon as the horse started to gallop."

"That's the only reason my legs felt numb?" she asked in an incredulous voice. Andrew thought she sounded like a frightened child, and it gave him some insight into what she must have lived through after the accident.

"That's right. A temporary sensation. You've got feeling in them now, haven't you?" He lifted the edge of the sheet and stroked the pads of her feet, causing Lindsay's legs to jump in reaction.

A stunned look crossed over her face and with some difficulty she sat up. Her gaze locked with Andrew's before flicking to the doctor's. "I can't believe it. I thought..."

"The injection we gave you has relaxed you," he explained. "Because of your past experience, fear made you tighten up, and that intensified the pain. I'm sending you home with a prescription for a muscle relaxant and an anti-inflammatory medication. You'll be sore for a while, but you're free to go as soon as you've dressed. Give yourself twelve hours before you resume your activities. A warm bath and bed rest will help."

Twelve hours to reach Lindsay and make her understand... Andrew shook the doctor's hand. "That's the news we wanted to hear."

The older man nodded and patted one of her legs. "When you're fully recovered, you can start doing exercises that use those muscles and eventually you can try horseback riding again. But take it in slow easy stages. That way you won't repeat today's experience. Good luck to you."

When the doctor left the cubicle, Andrew's first impulse was to take her in his arms. But he knew he couldn't do that. The woman who, earlier in the day, had admitted she wanted him beyond caution had become a totally different person. And he needed time to assimilate all she'd told him. "Would you like an attendant to come and help you dress?"

She gathered the sheet around her chin in what he assumed was a protective gesture. "Yes, please."

"When you're ready, the limo will be waiting at the emergency entrance."

She twisted the sheet in her hands convulsively. Avoiding his eyes, she said, "Thank you for everything. I feel like such a fraud."

"All I feel is relief that you'll be walking out of here on those beautiful legs of yours."

"Andrew—"

"Not now, Lindsay." He cut her off firmly and left the cubicle. He'd learned enough about her in the past few minutes to realize she'd try to avoid going home with him if she could. But this was one time she needed help, and he wanted to be the one to give it to her. If only he could get her to trust him. Then they could overcome this problem together, no matter how long it took.

"DAD? PUT LINDSAY in the bedroom next to mine. Then if she needs anything in the night, I can hear her."

"I promise I won't be bothering anybody," Lindsay murmured.

Andrew buried his lips in her hair. Her head rested beneath his chin as he carried her up the stairs to the second floor of the mansion. Her long golden hair cascaded over his arm like a waterfall. Though his natural instinct was to take her to the master bedroom, he suppressed that desire. Soon, however, she'd be sleeping in his bed—because, despite her fears, he intended to make her his wife.

"Since you won't be able to get back to coach your swim team in the morning, why don't you ask for a leave of absence and stay all month?" Randy asked excitedly. "We have a pool here where you can work out every day. And you can help Troy at the same time."

"That sounds like a wonderful idea, Randy, and I'm flattered you think I could help. But I'm afraid the owner of the swim club might have something to say about my taking another month off."

In the near future, Andrew mused, the owner of the club would have to find a permanent replacement. And the sooner the better. But he kept silent, secretly applauding his son. Randy was crazy about Lindsay and doing everything in his power to aid in the cause.

"Dad told me he invited you to come while Governor Stevens and his family are here on vacation. What's one more week? You wouldn't believe the fun stuff we've got planned," Randy went on.

Andrew carried her past Skip's post and into the room next to Randy's. He lowered her onto the quilted spread of one of the twin beds, aware he'd been holding his breath waiting for her answer. She refused to look at him and eased herself back against the pillow.

"Wonderful as it sounds, I'm afraid I have other commitments. But I feel honored that you'd even think of including me."

Andrew had something to say about that, but he'd wait until later when they were alone. Randy set her suitcase on the floor. "Are you hungry, Lindsay?"

"No. But I am thirsty."

"Do you want a soft drink or juice?"

"A Sprite or Seven-Up would taste good if you have it."

"Coming right up." Randy hurried out of the room, exchanging distress signals with his father before he disappeared.

The minute he left, Lindsay started to speak, but anticipating more rejection, Andrew took the initiative and headed for the connecting bathroom with her overnight bag. "The doctor said a soak in a hot tub would do you good," he called over his shoulder. "I'll turn on the taps and send in my housekeeper, Maud, to help you."

The bathroom had another door, which led to the hallway. Pretending he couldn't hear Lindsay's voice, he stepped into the corridor and intercepted Randy at the head of the stairs, taking the tumbler of Sprite from him. They communicated without words. "Thanks, son. Tell Maud to come up, will you?" Randy nodded and hurried off.

As soon as the tub was full, Andrew turned off the water and opened Lindsay's small case. Inside he found a cosmetic bag containing her toilet articles, as well as a blouse, some lingerie and a pair of light blue cotton pajamas. There was an intimacy in handling her personal effects that made him wish they were already married.

He laid everything out on the counter, then met Randy and the housekeeper outside Lindsay's room. Handing Maud the medicine he'd brought from the hospital pharmacy, he said, "Make sure she takes both pills with her drink before she gets into the tub. When she's through and presentable, come to my study and let me know. I'll take over from there. If she wants some dinner later, I'll get it."

Maud nodded. "It's nice to have a woman in the house again, Andrew."

"I've been thinking the same thing." They smiled with an easy camaraderie that had been achieved over five years of living through the best and worst together.

By tacit agreement, he and Randy went to the master bedroom. "Jeez, Dad. What are you going to do about Lindsay? She's not exactly cooperating."

"You noticed," he muttered. "I'm just going to have to keep her here until I can convince her that her fears about me are groundless."

"It's obvious she loves you, so I know you'll find a way."

He patted his son's shoulder. "I'm a fortunate man to have you in my corner. Now get out of here and enjoy yourself at the fireworks."

"I will. Troy and I are meeting those girls who posed as royalty on that float from the university."

"Sounds interesting. Just remember our five-minutes-to-say-good-night rule."

"No sweat. I've got to be at work by eight." He flashed his father a grin. "You behave yourself, too." His remark produced a weak smile from Andrew, lifting for a brief moment the black cloud that had settled over him.

After a quick shower and change of clothes, Andrew went downstairs to the kitchen. He made himself a sandwich and carried it to his study, where he phoned Clint. Emergencies happened on holidays, as well as workdays, and Andrew wanted to get any unfinished business out of the way before he went upstairs to check on Lindsay. Fortunately, though, it had been a quiet day, and he was free to concentrate on Lindsay.

It didn't matter what arguments she raised. Given more time, he'd overcome any obstacles. Tonight she would be sleeping in his home. Tomorrow they would spend the day together and he'd have his mermaid all to himself. They'd talk for hours, really talk. For now, that would be enough.

By the time Maud announced that Lindsay was in bed and resting comfortably, the study was cloaked in shadow. Andrew thanked his housekeeper, shoved aside the paperwork he hadn't touched and strode from the room. He took the stairs two at a time.

Maud had left Lindsay's door ajar. Andrew stepped inside the darkened room and with the stealth of a cat moved to the side of her bed. She lay with her back toward him, the sheet pulled to her waist.

He thought she must be asleep. After what she'd been through, it was only natural. But there was an uncivilized part of Andrew that wanted her awake and responsive to him. Swallowing his disappointment, he turned to leave.

"Andrew?"

His heart somersaulted and he wheeled around.

"Is that you?" she asked in a sluggish voice, rolling onto her back.

He moved closer. "I didn't mean to wake you. I only came in to make sure you were all right and to say good-night."

"I've been waiting." She sounded sedated. "We have to talk."

"Not tonight, Lindsay. Let the medication work. We've got all day tomorrow."

"No. You don't understand. I can't stay." The words came out slurred.

"You're not going anywhere until you're out of pain."

"The pain doesn't matter. I—"

But she didn't finish the rest of her sentence because a compulsion stronger than anything he'd ever felt before brought Andrew to his knees. He turned her onto her side, preventing her from talking. "Is this where it hurts?" he asked in a husky voice, gently massaging the sore area below her waist. The sheet remained in place.

She moaned in pleasure. "Oh . . . that feels good."

"It's supposed to." Unable to stop himself, he smoothed the long golden hair away from her shoulders and started to rub her back. With each circular motion of his hands he moved closer until his lips grazed the nape of her neck.

Somehow, without knowing how it happened, he found his hands touching the warm firm flesh where her pajamas had separated and the sheet had fallen away. A little gasp escaped her throat, the irresistible sound luring Andrew until his mouth found the corner of hers.

"Lindsay..." His voice shook with need.

In the next instant he had his heart's desire as she turned toward him again and raised her mouth to his.

Her passion in the barn was only a prelude to the breathtaking response she exhibited now. They kissed slowly, sensually, until Andrew was drowning in emotion. In sensation.

He didn't want to acknowledge that the pills had dulled her powers of thinking, allowing physical need to overrun conscious decisions. Before she'd been medicated, she'd all but told him there was no hope for a future together. Yet right now she welcomed him with unbridled passion, consumed by the fire they'd created.

She seemed oblivious to any pain, whispering his name over and over again. She couldn't seem to draw close enough to him, revealing a nature more loving, more giving, than any fantasy.

He'd been dreaming about moments like this ever since he'd first set eyes on her. But to make love to her when she wasn't in full command of her faculties, and when so much lay unresolved between them, went against his private code of ethics.

He pulled out of her arms and got to his feet. When he heard her groan of protest, he almost abandoned his principles and climbed into bed with her.

Holding on to his last vestige of self-control, he took a step back. On the way to the door he listened for her to whisper his name. That was all it would have taken; one word and he would have joined her for the night. But there was only silence.

Another few moments passed while he waited for some sign that she didn't want him to go. When it didn't come he forced himself to leave the room.

Skip looked up when he saw Andrew's tortured expression. "Is she all right?"

Andrew nodded. "The medicine has helped put her to sleep. I'm going to do some laps in the pool before I turn in. If she wakes up and needs me, you know where to find me."

"Right, Boss."

CHAPTER TEN

AROUND FOUR-THIRTY in the morning, Lindsay awoke from a nightmare. She was in a cold sweat, her pillow soaked with tears. She sat up in bed and pushed the damp hair out of her face.

She'd been dreaming about Andrew. They'd had some kind of horrible argument and he'd given her an ultimatum that resulted in their going their separate ways, lost to each other forever. The details of her dream were hazy, and half the time it was her father's image, her father's voice, rather than Andrew's, that tormented her. Nevertheless, a central theme had emerged from her subconscious mind and it confirmed her worst suspicion: marriage to Andrew would never work.

She had to get away from him before any lasting damage was done. She'd have left last evening if there'd been any way possible.

Though she still had soreness in her back, it wasn't nearly as bad as before and didn't impede her mobility. This much improvement meant she could leave the mansion without problem. According to the housekeeper, Andrew had taken the keys from Lindsay's purse and dispatched one of his men to Carson City to bring back her car. Had her keys been returned?

She reached for her purse on the bedside table and rummaged inside, fearing Andrew might still have them. When her fingers came in contact with the metal key ring, she felt ashamed for being so paranoid. It had occurred to her that he might have kept them until he felt she was well enough to drive. In the same situation, her father would have held on to them without a qualm, thinking as always that he knew what was best for her.

Lindsay had no idea when Andrew's day started, but she supposed that even if he was awake, he wouldn't be up yet. She'd learned enough about his security guards to know that, though they would be aware of her movements, they wouldn't interfere or prevent her from leaving. Her only problem was getting them to agree to say nothing to Andrew until she'd gone.

After making the bed, she hurried into the bathroom to get ready and to take the anti-inflammatory. Within ten minutes, she'd dressed in a fresh blouse and jeans and braided her hair. She was ready to go.

Before leaving the room, she sat down at the dressing table and wrote a note to Andrew, furiously wiping the tears from her cheeks. Only the urgent need to be far away from Carson City before he discovered her absence kept her from breaking down completely.

She thanked him for his generous hospitality and apologized for all the trouble she'd caused. With a trembling hand she reiterated what she'd told him in the emergency room—that a marriage between them would never work. It was better to part now, she wrote, before something happened that they'd both regret. She didn't want Randy hurt and asked Andrew to say goodbye to his son for her.

When she'd finished, she folded the paper and wrote his name on the front. Compulsively, she kissed the place where she'd written his name, then tucked the note in the corner of the mirror where it wouldn't be missed.

Maybe this was the coward's way out, but Lindsay knew she couldn't face him again. She didn't trust herself, not after the way she'd kissed him last night. When he touched her she lost the ability to think. That was the problem. They couldn't be near each other without ending up in each other's arms.

The moment he'd come upstairs to check on her, he'd started to massage the ache in her back. She could no more refuse him than stop breathing. Much as she wanted to blame the medicine for her uninhibited response to his caresses, she knew that wasn't the truth.

The ecstasy of his kiss had sent her over the edge. All she'd wanted to do was make love with him. If it hadn't been for his strength of will, they would have spent the rest of the night together. She'd be tempting fate if she allowed this situation to go on any longer.

After one more glance around the charming bedroom with its floral wallpaper, its cedar wainscoting and old-fashioned lamps, she gathered up her hat and purse. Clutching the overnight bag in her other hand, she tiptoed into the darkened hallway and headed for the wide elegant staircase.

The only light came from two ornate wall sconces near the top of the stairs. After passing Randy's room, she caught sight of a new security guard seated on a chair near the railing, reading a book. The man was blond and well built. She took another step closer, then let out a shocked gasp when she realized who it was.

"So my instincts were correct, after all," he said coldly.

When he finally looked up at her, it was an Andrew she barely recognized. She felt as if the earth had suddenly veered off on a different course, knocking her sideways. His features had hardened; his expression was uncompromising, unrelenting.

He hurled the book down the corridor, uncaring of the noise it made, and the action underlined the extent of his rage. Right now his eyes resembled black ice. She had a strong conviction they'd never again look at her with passion or love.

A sound from behind made her whirl around. Randy was standing in the hall in his pajamas. "What's going on?" he asked.

So many conflicting emotions gripped her she couldn't speak.

"I'm glad you're awake," Andrew said in clipped tones directly behind her. "Our mermaid was just leaving."

Randy blinked in total bewilderment, twisting Lindsay's emotions even more. "Why, Lindsay? It's the middle of the night."

"That's right, son. But we'll forgive her because she's an underwater creature who likes the dark—where she can slither in and out of crevices and remain undetected by humans."

Lindsay gasped again. The hurt she'd never meant to inflict on Andrew had gone marrow-deep.

"You're in time to bid her a final farewell before she disappears to her underwater world. You see, she prefers the company of sharks, who neither love nor hate, who leave mermaids alone and never make demands of any kind—except when there's no other meal to be had."

Lindsay listened in horror as the bitterness continued to pour out of Andrew. She'd killed every bit of feeling in him and would have to live with the consequences of her actions for the rest of her life.

"I-I'm sorry," she whispered to both of them, shaking her head, wishing she could die. Her mouth was so dry she could hardly make a sound.

"I'm sorry, too," Randy murmured, his eyes suspiciously bright. "Dad and I thought it would be cool to capture a mermaid, but I guess what they say about salvage is wrong. Some things under the water are better left there. Goodbye, Lindsay." His voice held a telltale tremor. "See you on TV." He went back to his room and shut the door, and the echo seemed to resound in her heart.

"Legend has it that mermaids lead sailors to their doom. I always wondered where that belief came from. Now I know."

She turned around, desperate to make Andrew understand. "Please. Listen to me. There's something about me you don't know. It has to do with my parents and the way they've always tried to control me. My life became a prison, and things got so bad I went to a therapist. He helped me learn how to deal with them."

His eyes cut like knives. "My congratulations to your therapist. His cure is a hundred percent effective. Just cut off all human contact." His voice was heavy with sarcasm. "Any fool knows it's impossible to turn a mermaid into a woman. I found out the hard way and have the scars to prove it." His mouth became a white line of anger. "The spell is broken, the enchantment's, over. Go back to your underwater world where you're free of mortal ties. Where you're free of a man with his less than perfect instinct to cherish and protect the women in his life. You and I have nothing more to say to each other."

"Andrew!" she cried from her heart, so confused that she no longer knew what she felt, what she thought. "I swear I didn't mean to hurt you!"

"I believe you." His voice sounded remote and empty. "From the first day you did everything in your power to warn me off." After a brief pause, he said, "Consider me warned."

Turning from her, he called to the man Lindsay could see positioned at the bottom of the staircase. "Larry? Please show Ms. Marshall to her car, then bring around the limo for me. I'm due in Las Vegas for a meeting at seven."

For the second time in her life, Lindsay could tell she was drowning. But this time no diver stood by to come to her rescue. *She was on her own...*

"BETH?"

The lovely brunette, who bore a striking resemblance to her actress mother, swiveled around in her office chair. She took one look at Lindsay and said, "I guess two hours late is better than not coming at all. Good heavens, could this really be the gorgeous mermaid everyone in the United States is talking about?

Sit down before you fall down." She jumped up from her desk. "I'll get you something to drink."

"No. Please don't bother. I couldn't touch anything right now."

Beth shut the door to give them privacy, then sat down again and regarded her friend anxiously. "You had a purpose when you called me this morning. What's really going on with you?"

Lindsay lowered her head. "I shouldn't have come here and bothered you at work."

"I don't know why not. How many times in our lives have I run next door to your house in hysterics because one of mother's husbands had been caught with another woman—or made a pass at me? Lindsay, don't you know that if it wasn't for you, I'd have lost my sanity years ago? You never bother me. That's the trouble."

"What do you mean?" Lindsay whispered, lifting a tear-ravaged face.

"Don't pretend you don't know what I'm talking about. I'm Beth, remember? Do you realize we've only talked a couple of times since you came back from Carson City last month? And not once have you mentioned Andrew or what happened."

More tears gushed from Lindsay's eyes. "I couldn't."

"That's obvious, so I've had to resort to the next best thing, which is watching your TV commercial. It's sensational. My mother says you've been approached to do a new live-action film of *The Little Mermaid.*"

Lindsay nodded. "That's the last thing I want to do. Unfortunately my agent won't leave me alone. He's been hounding my parents to talk me into doing it."

"That was a fatal mistake," Beth murmured. "He should have come to me—I'd have set him straight." She sat back in the swivel chair, crossing her arms. "Is your job at the club finished?"

"Yes. Yesterday was my last day."

"So, when are you leaving for San Diego?"

The silence stretched endlessly. "I don't want to go to San Diego," Lindsay admitted in a small voice.

"Hallelujah! When did it finally dawn on you that you never really wanted to be a marine biologist?"

Lindsay stared at her friend. "On the drive home from Carson City. Oh, Beth—" she shook her head "—you were so right about me. All along I've been punishing Andrew for things that never had anything to do with him. I accused him of crimes he could never commit. He isn't anything like Dad, but I was so blinded by my fears I wouldn't listen to him. Now it's too late. I've lost him. Really lost him." Her voice wavered with renewed grief.

"That's what you said before, and you were wrong."

"Not this time." Too restless to sit, she paced the floor. "If you think I did the unforgivable when Andrew came to see me in Culver City, it's nothing compared to the way I treated him and Randy over the Fourth of July." She paused long enough to catch her breath. "He asked me to marry him. But in the emergency room I threw his proposal ba—"

"Just a minute," Beth broke in. "I'm going to put my Do Not Disturb sign on the door and ask Janet to take my calls. Then I want to hear this from the very beginning."

Once Beth had returned to her office, Lindsay found herself revealing the details of her visit to Carson City, the terrifying episode in the hospital, the horror of that night at the mansion when she'd thought she could escape Andrew without having to face him.

She buried her wet face in her hands. "He said things to me that still hurt. And the wounded look in Randy's eyes . . . I'll never forget any of it."

Beth leaned forward, clasping her hands on top of the desk. "How much do you love him?"

Wiping the moisture from her cheeks, Lindsay said, "Enough to do *anything* to win back his love. I know now that nothing in the world matters if I can't live the rest of my life with him." Her voice grew steadier. "That's why I'm here. I have a plan and I want to know what you think of it."

Lindsay could see the blaze of interest mixed with surprise in Beth's eyes, and it prompted her to say, "It's ludicrous and outrageous, and if it fails, I really will have lost Andrew forever—not to mention that I'll be the laughingstock of Nevada, if not the whole country. But I'm willing to risk any humiliation, undergo any sacrifice, to make him understand what he means to me."

Slowly Beth rose to her feet, a smile growing on her face. "Is this the same Lindsay I've known for the last twenty years?"

"No. Because of Andrew, that Lindsay died on her way back to California last month. I'm not exactly sure who the new Lindsay Marshall is, but I know she wants to be Andrew Cordell's wife."

"Well, what do you know. Let's hear about this little scheme of yours."

"First of all I need to talk to Randy. He and Andrew are very close, and I hurt him when I hurt his father. If he can't forgive me, then I know there's no hope." Her voice trembled on the last few words.

"Okay," Beth said practically. "Let's assume that he'll be overjoyed to find out you want to be his stepmother. Now tell me what you're going to do before I die of curiosity."

Without further hesitation, Lindsay spelled it out. When she'd explained everything, Beth's eyes gleamed and she picked up the phone, handing it to Lindsay. "Call Randy at work right now. Catch him off guard while Andrew's not around."

Buoyed by Beth's unqualified approval, Lindsay called Carson City information for the number, then phoned the scuba-diving shop.

"Dives and Divers," a woman's voice answered.

"May I speak to Randy Cordell, please?" she asked as Beth signaled that she was leaving the office to her.

"Hold on a minute. I think he's out at the pool."

Lindsay sat in Beth's chair, clutching the receiver tightly in her hand.

"Randy Cordell."

Lindsay's mouth went dry. "Randy?"

"Jeez . . ." she heard him murmur. *"Lindsay?"*

"Yes. Please don't hang up."

"Why would I do that?"

She blinked. "I thought you must despise me as much as your father does."

"What in the heck are you talking about?"

"I was cruel to your father. I hurt him deeply without meaning to."

"Yeah. I know." His quiet comment confirmed her greatest fear.

"How is he?"

"Busier than ever."

She suspected as much. "Did Governor Stevens and his family come for that visit?"

"Yeah. Troy and I had a lot of fun with his daughters. Dad and Jim spent time riding and talking shop."

Lindsay closed her eyes tightly. "Did you go on that scuba-diving trip to the Caymans like the two of you planned?"

"No. Dad said he's had his fill of underwater adventure, so we camped out at Hidden Lake with Uncle Zack and Troy. We just got back yesterday, as a matter of fact."

Taking the plunge, she said, "Randy, does he ever talk about me?"

"No. He can't even sit through one of your commercials. A few weeks ago at the ranch while we were all watching TV, he got up and left the house when it came on."

Lindsay's heart pounded so hard it hurt. "Randy, did you know your father asked me to marry him?"

"Yeah. Why did you turn him down, Lindsay?" he asked, and she could hear the hurt in his voice.

"Because...because I had some things to work out first."

"I could have sworn you loved him."

"I did. I do. More than anything in the world."

"Then what's the problem?"

Her eyes filled. "There isn't one. Not anymore."

After a slight pause he asked, "What did you say?" the excitement in his voice was almost palpable. The difference between his tone earlier and now was like night and day.

"I want to marry him as soon as possible, if he'll still have me. I'd like us to be a family."

Jeez! You're not kidding, are you?" His happy shouts were like old familiar music.

"No, I'm not. Is that good or bad?" she teased.

"It's *fantastic!*"

"Except for one thing," Lindsay said quietly. "Your father told me to go back where I came from, that we had nothing more to say to each other. You heard him and you know he meant it."

"That's because he fell in love with you the minute he first saw you swimming at 20,000 Leagues. He couldn't take it when you turned him down."

"I need another chance to ask his forgiveness and convince him we should be together. Permanently. Will you help me?"

"What do you think?"

"I think I love you very much, Randy Cordell."

"Yeah. The feeling's mutual."

CHAPTER ELEVEN

WHEN HE SAW Randy peek into his office at the capitol, Andrew waved him inside. "I don't care what he says, Clint. I want that report on my desk first thing in the morning or I'm going to call for a public audit. You can quote me on that!"

"It's a good thing Aunt Alex invited us for dinner. You sound hungry," Randy said teasingly after his father slammed down the receiver. "I bet you skipped lunch again today."

"There hasn't been time." Andrew got up from his desk and shrugged into his suit jacket, aware that he'd lost interest in a lot of things since Linday's flight from his life. "We've uncovered graft at the retirement-fund office. Now that the media's gotten wind of it, I want to be ten jumps ahead of them."

"Sounds serious. Is that why there's a big crowd out front on the steps? I had trouble getting in."

"It's probably a bunch of tourists taking a group picture." Andrew reached for his briefcase and filled it with the latest incriminating reports. He planned to spike his guns before morning.

"There's a television crew out there, too."

Andrew flashed a surprised glance at Randy before buzzing his press secretary. Moments later she hurried into the room. "What's going on out front, Judith? Randy saw some newspeople, including TV crews."

"According to Jake, there's some TV celebrity in town planning to make a statement. You've been challenged to come outside to hear it, but I think this is one time you should bow out. That's why I decided not to bother you with it."

Andrew flashed her a wicked smile. "You know me better than that, Judith. The press is waiting for me to back down on the retirement-fund scandal. I have an idea that's what this is all about."

"Go for it, Dad! Nobody thinks faster on their feet than you do."

"Thanks for the vote of confidence, Randy."

Judith didn't look convinced. "I don't know. I don't like it."

"Tell Jake to alert the others. Whoever's behind this latest scam must be desperate to pull a stunt like this. Well, I'm up to the challenge."

"Governor, why don't we let Clint handle it?"

"No. Whoever it is has walked into my parlor. Let's be hospitable and accommodate him," Andrew reasoned, feeling that spurt of adrenaline that preceded a heated debate.

He loved nothing more than to sink his teeth into the heart of a conflict. For a little while it helped him to forget that he was a man with needs and desires only one woman could fulfill. *But she was lost to him.* Maybe one day in the distant future, if the gods were kind, he would be granted the gift of forgetfulness.... "Shall we go, Randy?"

"Yeah. Aunt Alex won't be too mad when she finds out why we're late."

Andrew followed his son out the door and through the rotundâ to the main entry. He was surprised at the size of the crowd that had gathered. Someone had been busy. Spectators overflowed onto the driveway and grounds. Jake nodded to Andrew. "We're ready when you are, Governor."

"Lead the way."

A path cleared as Andrew walked out the doors of the capitol, surrounded by his security men. But when he caught sight of the voluptuous mermaid draped luxuriously across the top step, smiling and waving to the delight of a wolf-whistling crowd, he felt as if he'd just slammed into an invisible wall. He gripped his son's shoulder.

The blazing sun glinted off her molten gold hair and metallic tail, dazzling his eyes. Her back was toward him, so she couldn't see him standing there. He doubted anyone in the crowd noticed him, either. Her one-piece mermaid costume, which fit her long-legged curvaceous body like a layer of skin, drew the eye of every spectator around and made it a literal impossibility for Andrew to look anywhere else.

"Good evening, ladies and gentlemen in our viewing audience," a reporter said into the camera. She stood a couple of steps above the mermaid. "Tonight we're bringing you a special news exclusive from the steps of our historic capitol building here in Carson City.

"Last June, you will recall that our governor, Andrew Cordell, made headlines when he went to the Bahamas and met a breathtaking mermaid while scuba diving with his son.

"This evening, a source who wishes to remain unidentified informed us that the mysterious mermaid—who's become the country's overnight sensation as the lovely television star for Beauty from the Sea cosmetics—was lying here on the steps of the capitol protesting unfair treatment." She bent over to address the mermaid. "Would you elaborate for our television audience what you mean? What exactly are you protesting? And why?"

"Hey, Dad, go easy on my shoulder," Randy whispered, but Andrew wasn't aware of his own strength or anything else, because Lindsay, who had pulled herself into a sitting position, started to speak.

"Well, it all began when I was swimming around in my own world, minding my own business. Suddenly this...this *mortal* appeared and he refused to leave me alone."

"You mean Governor Cordell?"

"Yes," she said, producing an appreciative chuckle from the crowd, some of whom had finally realized that Andrew had come outside to watch and listen.

"I was afraid, because where I come from it's the law to stay away from mortals. My parents raised me to be very obedient and never let a mortal get close enough to capture me."

"Are you telling the audience that the governor captured you against your will?"

"He did something much worse." At that comment, Randy elbowed his father in the ribs, but Andrew stood there as rigid as the granite pillar next to him. "When I was in danger, he saved my life."

"That sounds like something our governor would do. He's a great supporter of women's rights. Why are you so upset?"

"Because once a mermaid has physical contact with a mortal, her power to resist him is weakened. She no longer listens to her parents and finds opportunities to be with this mortal all the time—until it's too late."

"Too late? I don't think we understand."

"You see, a mermaid's greatest fear is becoming enslaved by a mortal, falling under his power. Once that happens, a mermaid isn't content with her life under the sea anymore."

"Is that what happened to you?"

"Yes. When this mortal asked me to live with him forever and never return to my own world, I panicked because everything my parents taught me had come true. This mortal wanted to capture me and hold me and never let me go."

"Did he use force with you?"

"Oh, no! He did something much more powerful."

"And what was that?"

"He said he was in love with me."

A roar went up from the crowd, but the blood pounding in Andrew's ears made everything sound muffled.

"I was so frightened I started to swim away. That's when he hurt me."

"Our governor hurt you? What did he do?"

"He got angry. I didn't know he could get like that because he'd always been kind and gentle."

Andrew staggered from the anguish in her voice and felt the casing of ice around his heart begin to crack.

"He told me to go back where I came from, that we had nothing more to say to each other."

"But isn't that what you wanted? To be free?"

"Oh no! You see, I *thought* I wanted to be free, because all my life I've been taught to stay away from mortals. But when I returned to the sea, I became desolate and cried all the time. I discovered I didn't want to be on my own, constantly having to protect myself from sharks and other sea creatures."

She lifted her head and looked directly into the camera. "I want to put my tail away and be a mortal like him. I want to live with this mortal forever and ever, but I also want to help serve others. The problem is, I've been a mermaid so long I can only do one thing well. So I've thought of a plan. I have to know if you think it will work."

"Our viewers would love to hear your plan. I'm sure."

"Well, you see, all mermaids have jobs to do. Mine has been to teach baby mermaids how to swim. Some of them are born with oddly shaped tails, and some of them run into jagged coral. When that happens, they need special swimming lessons so their tails will grow strong and they can keep up with the others.

"If I become a mortal with legs, the only thing I'll be allowed to bring with me from the sea is my talent for teaching others how to swim. The mortal I love has a great big swimming pool. So I thought if I could help teach swimming to little mortals with legs that are oddly shaped or hurt, then he'll let me stay with him, and we'll work side by side and be happy."

"I'm sure when he hears about your plan, he'll be very happy and never let you go."

"Oh, I hope so. You see, I always dreamed of having a baby mermaid of my own to teach. Now all I can dream about is having a baby mortal of my own. His little mortal. But I'm afraid that will never happen."

The crowd made commiserating sounds. The reporter asked, "Because the Governor doesn't want you anymore? Is that what you're saying?"

"Yes. I've been waiting at all our familiar haunts, hoping to catch sight of him. But he's never come for me," she said with tears in her voice. "That's why I'm here. I tried to make it as far as his office, but I've lost all my powers as a mermaid and . . . and I collapsed as I reached the top step. Unless he claims me for his own, I'll never turn into a real woman with legs."

"You mean you'll have to stay just as you are?"

"Yes. Unable to return to the sea and unable to walk. It's the cruelest punishment of all."

"Shame on the governor. You have every right to protest. What would you like the television audience to do?"

"Well, I've heard that his constituents can call in when they feel strongly about an issue. I was hoping that if everyone heard my story, they'd take pity on me and beg the governor on my behalf. I have nowhere to go. Nowhere to turn."

"I think we ought to stage an all-night protest right here on the steps!" Randy shouted to the crowd, eliciting cheers of approval as he left Andrew's side to join the mermaid.

Andrew closed his eyes tightly, too overcome with emotion to move. It came to him then.

Lindsay loved him.

She loved him enough to win his son's affection and support. And his help. She wanted to marry Andrew enough to humble herself in front of thousands of people. In exposing herself, she'd taken a risk he hadn't thought her capable of.

When he opened his eyes, he stared in disbelief. Troy and Alex, along with Zack who was carrying Sean in his arms, had joined Lindsay and Randy. *Everyone he loved was here.*

"Hey, Boss?" Jake murmured. "Are you going to pick her up and carry her off, or do you want one of us to do it?"

A smile broke the corner of Andrew's mouth. "If you lay one finger on her, you're fired!" Then he started walking toward Lindsay.

The reporter met him halfway and held the mike in front of him. "Well, Governor? It looks like you've got a problem sitting on your doorstep. The crowd is growing bigger and more unruly. What do you intend to do about it?"

He looked past the reporter to Lindsay, who had turned around. The violet blue eyes staring up at him were so haunted, so full of anxiety, he realized she wasn't at all certain of his answer.

She'd laid every bit of human pride on the line for him. He felt so humbled by her action he could scarcely find the words.

"Governor?" the reporter prompted.

Zack moved in and whispered, "Even you know when your number is up, brother. It happens to all of us. Give in graciously."

Andrew cleared his throat and faced the camera, afraid to look at Lindsay again until they were alone.

Seven weeks had gone by since he'd held her. Seven bleak, meaningless weeks that felt more like seven years.

"Last fall," he began, "when I was voted in for a second term, I didn't know a certain mermaid would swim into my life and turn it into chaos. Take it from me, mermaids are elusive creatures." The crowd chuckled.

"They beckon, then retreat. To defend himself against such torment, a mortal has to do something to protect his fragile heart from being dashed to pieces against the rocks."

"But, Governor," said the reporter, "if the television audience understands the situation correctly, she's no longer a mermaid and wants to be a mortal woman. In fact, she'll be caught between both worlds if you don't do something about it."

Steeling himself not to look at Lindsay, he said, "Then by all means let's put it to a vote before my opponents accuse me of deliberately disturbing the environment and destroying an endangered species." The chuckles turned into full-scale laughter.

"How many of my constituents out there would like to see this ex-mermaid become the first lady of the state of Nevada?"

A deafening cheer arose from the crowd. When it finally quieted down, the reporter said, "I think we can safely say you've been given a mandate, Governor..." She paused. "Governor?"

But Andrew had done all the talking he intended to do. While the newswoman wound up the television segment, Andrew took the steps needed to reach

Lindsay, whose face radiated the same excitement and joy exploding inside him.

He leaned down and whispered, "Put your arms around my neck, darling." Lindsay did, and he scooped her up against his heart, burying his face in her neck. "You've done it now, my reluctant mermaid. You're trapped on dry land with me and there's no going back."

She wriggled closer in response, fanning the flame that blazed out of control. "Then take me someplace where we can be alone and I can shed my tail. I love you, Andrew Cordell, and I need to show you how I feel before I burst."

He understood exactly how she felt. His own emotions had transcended mere words and needed physical expression. Even then, he might never be satisfied.

Holding her tight against him, he headed for his private office inside the capitol, while his security men shielded them from the crush of curious onlookers.

But even before the door to his private office closed, shutting out the rest of the world, Lindsay's mouth covered his with possessive force, changing the rhythm of his runaway heart forever. Starved for each other, they kissed with increasing passion, abandoning all restraints. When the rap on the door sounded, Andrew was too wrapped up in what he was doing to respond.

"Hey, Dad? I hate to break the news, but your five minutes are up. Remember our rule."

"That's a terrible rule," Lindsay whispered against his lips and clutched him tighter. "Who made it?"

Andrew groaned. "I did. But it was only supposed to be for Randy."

"Dad?"

"Go away, son."

"I can't do that. This is for your own good. Besides Aunt Alex and Uncle Zack, everyone on the staff, plus photographers from a couple of newspapers, are waiting in the rotunda to meet Lindsay. It could get embarrassing if you don't make an appearance soon. I'll give you one more minute. And while I'm counting, keep in mind that you owe me and Troy a trip to the Caymans. We were thinking that's where we ought to go for your honeymoon."

BETH HAD HELPED Lindsay change out of her wedding dress and into her going-away suit at least half an hour ago, and still Andrew hadn't shown up. When her anxiety level had reached its peak, Beth volunteered to find out what had detained him.

Lindsay finally heard her husband's deep voice call to her from the hallway, and she dashed to the door, flinging it open. "At last!" she cried, drawing him inside. "I was afraid something was wrong."

Except for her father, no man had ever entered the bedroom her mother had decorated to suit a little girl's tastes. Andrew's tall virile body, clothed in an expensive smoky blue suit, looked incongruous among the frilly decor.

He cupped her flushed face in his hands and lifted it for his inspection. "What could possibly go wrong on our wedding night?"

"I...I don't know," she whispered nervously. "I saw Daddy take you aside after we finished greeting all the wedding guests, and I've been worried ever since. Zack drove Troy and Randy to the airport at least twenty minutes ago. Aren't we going to be too late to board our plane?"

He lowered his head and kissed her. "Don't worry, darling. There's still time and this was important. Your parents and I have just had an illuminating conversation."

His explanation filled her with fresh anxiety. "What do you mean?"

"Helen and Ned wanted me to know how grateful they were that I'd influenced you to have the wedding at home."

"But—"

"Hear me out," he murmured, and smothered the rest of her protest with his lips. "They assumed I had to coerce you into letting them be a part of things. They admitted that relations between the three of you haven't been good for a long time. In fact, when you and I phoned them a month ago to tell them we were getting married, they figured they'd lost you completely. They even intimated it was their fault."

"They did?" Lindsay was incredulous.

Andrew nodded and kissed her palms. "When I told them I had nothing to do with the decision to let them plan our wedding, that it was entirely your idea and that you did it because you love them, it had a real effect on them. Your mother broke down and your father became... subdued."

"Daddy? Subdued? I can't imagine my father ever letting anyone else have the last word." Her voice shook.

"It's clear they love you, and it's beginning to dawn on them that if they want to see us often and get to know the children we're planning to have, then they've got to let you live your own life. They've got to stop issuing ultimatums and start giving you more credit for loving them back, or they really will lose you. Lindsay, it's a step in the right direction."

"I agree. Oh, Andrew..." She flung her arms around his neck and lifted her eyes to his. "It's your unselfishness and perceptions about people that have brought about this change in them. How could I be so blessed to have married a man like you?"

"I was just thinking the same thing about my new wife," he said in a husky tone. "Though he hoped you'd understand he was just teasing, Randy did want to come with us on our honeymoon. Ever since Wendie's health started to really fail, he's lost confidence in life and in the future. He's felt broken.

"When you asked him if he'd like to fly to the Caymans with us and bring Troy, you put the pieces of his life back together and re-created that sense of family. You let him know he belonged. Lindsay—" Andrew's body trembled "—when you did that, I swear I fell in love with you all over again."

Then he grinned. "Just don't plan on joining the boys for any underwater sports. This time is for us. And much as you love swimming, I have something else in mind that's going to keep us fully occupied. Maybe on rare occasions we'll surface for dinner."

But Lindsay was way ahead of him and kissed the man she loved with uninhibited passion. "Maybe not even then, Andrew Cordell." She kissed him a second time. "Maybe not even then."

brings you

Stories that celebrate love, families and children!

Watch for our first Kids & Kisses

The Baby Battle
by Shannon Waverly
Harlequin Romance #3316

A deeply emotional Romance centering on the custody battle for a young boy.

Who will be four-year-old Timmy's guardian?

His aunt, Suzanna, who was his mother's sister?

Or his uncle, Logan, a member of the powerful New England family who'd disowned Timmy's father?

Available in June wherever Harlequin books are sold.

KIDS1

INDULGE A LITTLE 6947 SWEEPSTAKES
NO PURCHASE NECESSARY

HERE'S HOW THE SWEEPSTAKES WORKS:
The Harlequin Reader Service shipments for January, February and March 1994 will contain, respectively, coupons for entry into three prize drawings: a trip for two to San Francisco, an Alaskan cruise for two and a trip for two to Hawaii. To be eligible for any drawing using an Entry Coupon, simply complete and mail according to directions.

There is no obligation to continue as a Reader Service subscriber to enter and be eligible for any prize drawing. You may also enter any drawing by hand printing your name and address on a 3" x 5" card and the destination of the prize you wish that entry to be considered for (i.e., San Francisco trip, Alaskan cruise or Hawaiian trip). Send your 3" x 5" entries to: Indulge a Little 6947 Sweepstakes, c/o Prize Destination you wish that entry to be considered for, P.O. Box 1315, Buffalo, NY 14269-1315, U.S.A. or Indulge a Little 6947 Sweepstakes, P.O. Box 610, Fort Erie, Ontario L2A 5X3, Canada.

To be eligible for the San Francisco trip, entries must be received by 4/30/94; for the Alaskan cruise, 5/31/94; and the Hawaiian trip, 6/30/94. No responsibility is assumed for lost, late or misdirected mail. Sweepstakes open to residents of the U.S. (except Puerto Rico) and Canada, 18 years of age or older. All applicable laws and regulations apply. Sweepstakes void wherever prohibited.

For a copy of the Official Rules, send a self-addressed, stamped envelope (WA residents need not affix return postage) to: Indulge a Little 6947 Rules, P.O. Box 4631, Blair, NE 68009, U.S.A.

INDR93

INDULGE A LITTLE 6947 SWEEPSTAKES
NO PURCHASE NECESSARY

HERE'S HOW THE SWEEPSTAKES WORKS:
The Harlequin Reader Service shipments for January, February and March 1994 will contain, respectively, coupons for entry into three prize drawings: a trip for two to San Francisco, an Alaskan cruise for two and a trip for two to Hawaii. To be eligible for any drawing using an Entry Coupon, simply complete and mail according to directions.

There is no obligation to continue as a Reader Service subscriber to enter and be eligible for any prize drawing. You may also enter any drawing by hand printing your name and address on a 3" x 5" card and the destination of the prize you wish that entry to be considered for (i.e., San Francisco trip, Alaskan cruise or Hawaiian trip). Send your 3" x 5" entries to: Indulge a Little 6947 Sweepstakes, c/o Prize Destination you wish that entry to be considered for, P.O. Box 1315, Buffalo, NY 14269-1315, U.S.A. or Indulge a Little 6947 Sweepstakes, P.O. Box 610, Fort Erie, Ontario L2A 5X3, Canada.

To be eligible for the San Francisco trip, entries must be received by 4/30/94; for the Alaskan cruise, 5/31/94; and the Hawaiian trip, 6/30/94. No responsibility is assumed for lost, late or misdirected mail. Sweepstakes open to residents of the U.S. (except Puerto Rico) and Canada, 18 years of age or older. All applicable laws and regulations apply. Sweepstakes void wherever prohibited.

For a copy of the Official Rules, send a self-addressed, stamped envelope (WA residents need not affix return postage) to: Indulge a Little 6947 Rules, P.O. Box 4631, Blair, NE 68009, U.S.A.

INDR93

INDULGE A LITTLE

SWEEPSTAKES

OFFICIAL ENTRY COUPON

This entry must be received by: APRIL 30, 1994
This month's winner will be notified by: MAY 15, 1994
Trip must be taken between: JUNE 30, 1994-JUNE 30, 1995

YES, I want to win the San Francisco vacation for two. I understand that the prize includes round-trip airfare, first-class hotel, rental car and pocket money as revealed on the "wallet" scratch-off card.

Name____________________

Address ____________________ Apt. __________

City____________________

State/Prov.__________ Zip/Postal Code__________

Daytime phone number____________________
(Area Code)

Account #____________________

Return entries with invoice in envelope provided. Each book in this shipment has two entry coupons—and the more coupons you enter, the better your chances of winning!

 MONTH1

INDULGE A LITTLE

SWEEPSTAKES

OFFICIAL ENTRY COUPON

This entry must be received by: APRIL 30, 1994
This month's winner will be notified by: MAY 15, 1994
Trip must be taken between: JUNE 30, 1994-JUNE 30, 1995

YES, I want to win the San Francisco vacation for two. I understand that the prize includes round-trip airfare, first-class hotel, rental car and pocket money as revealed on the "wallet" scratch-off card.

Name____________________

Address ____________________ Apt. __________

City____________________

State/Prov.__________ Zip/Postal Code__________

Daytime phone number____________________
(Area Code)

Account #____________________

Return entries with invoice in envelope provided. Each book in this shipment has two entry coupons—and the more coupons you enter, the better your chances of winning!

© 1993 HARLEQUIN ENTERPRISES LTD. MONTH1